DEATH FROM ABOVE!

SCOUNDRELS of the WASTELAND #3

J.I. GRECO

WHOLESALE
ATOMICS

ISBN: 9781980427766

Published by Wholesale Atomics.

DEATH FROM ABOVE!

CHAPTER ONE

THE STEAM-POWERED 1976 Volkswagen Beetle skitters across the snow-covered tundra of the Florida panhandle on six piston-driven, snow-shoe footed legs.

"Nah, no way. How do you even get to there?" Inside the Beetle and bundled up warm in a fur-lined parka, Roxanne is driving from the passenger seat over wireless connection via her cybernetic implant, her belly too big now to fit safely behind the wheel. "Two o'clock," she says with the slightest jog of her head.

"On it," Bernie says from the back seat. She shifts, slowly, trying to keep her own bulky parka from rustling loud enough to wake the three month old Jake asleep in his sling under her left arm or interrupt his twin brother Finn's second breakfast at her right nipple. She slips the barrel of the pump-action rail-pistol out a window. "You've been watching the same episodes I have. How could you not get there? It's not even subtext. It's just there. Blatant." Casually squinting down the short barrel, Bernie lines up her shot and thumbs the trigger. A soft electric *ptztzzz*, the slightest of oily puffs of aerosolized lubricant sprouting from the barrel tip, and three-hundred meters off to their right, a clean thumb-sized hole appears in the domed head of one of the three-wheeled dronemobiles that have been swarming at them ever since they'd broken through the razor-wire perimeter fence surrounding the compound. Its semi-AI brainpan ruptured, the dronemobile jerks to a sudden halt, faceplanting into a snowbank.

"I can't see it." Her head filled with telemetric ghost-images from the Bug's sensor array, Roxanne keeps most of her attention on a bump just over the next ridge that could be another dronemobile, hiding in wait. Or maybe it's just a fallen tree trunk under two feet of blue-white snow. *Guess we're just gonna have to drive over it to find out,* Roxanne thinks, twisting around to frown at Bernice. "I mean, it was a different time back then—like, nuns had to swear loyalty to men, you believe that bullshit? Anyway, old people didn't have sex. They had laws against that sort of thing."

Bernice takes a depleted uranium slug from the diaper bag on the floorboard and shoves it into a slot in the side of the rail-pistol's barrel. "I'm telling you, they were doing it, laws be damned. Like rabbits. Like dirty, octogenarian rabbits."

"Sweet little old Mrs. Fletcher and Doc Hazlitt were not fucking." Roxanne's nose twitches, sending a signal to the Bug to leap over the ridge and that downed-tree/hiding dronemobile. "Releasing," she warns as the Bug passes over the lump and her nose twitches again, this time telling the Bug to release a small contact cluster bomb from a compartment in its belly, just in case the bump in the ridge isn't a downed tree.

Turns out, it's not.

The bomb hits the lump just as the dronemobile emerges from its hiding place and shakes the layer of snow off its dome.

"They were just old friends," Roxanne says. "Platonic friends. Besides, when did she ever have time to do it? Everywhere she went another corpse showed up that needed investigating."

"During commercial breaks, probably. Bet they even had threesomes with Sheriff Tupper every other Tuesday—" Bernice clamps her hands over Jake's little ears as the Bug lands deftly on its front feet and behind it the bomb goes *BOOM!*, throwing up a crown of snow and chunks of dronemobile. At her breast, Finn just keeps sucking. "And at Thanksgiving, all three of them would pass around her nephew Grady and the Turkey basting bulb for a little anal humiliation action."

"You are absolutely destroying the rose-colored image I have of our ancestral pre-apocalyptic past, I hope you know." The Bug idling at the top of the ridge, Roxanne closes her eyes and sweeps the horizon with the car's sensors. No more autodrone blips, or even the hint of a possible one. "Think that was the last of them," she says, opening her eyes and prodding the Bug to begin slowly prancing down the hill with a twitch of her nose. "I wish I'd never found those DVD boxed-sets in the landfill."

"I'm glad you did," Bernice says. "I need something to do while these little bastards are sucking me dry, don't I?"

"Shatner, they didn't even bother mining the perimeter," Roxanne turns to look out the Bug's front windshield, down at the double-wide mobile home up on cinder blocks at the bottom of the hill. The sensors don't show her anything buried under the snow around it. *No explosives, anyway.* Snow drifts are piled up against the northern side, all the way up to the roof. Black smoke pours out of a bent chimney. The windows are taped over with layer on layer of newspaper. The hood of a Dodge *Swinger*, its heavily armored skin pock-marked with rust and the dents of small, and not so small, arms damage, pokes out from behind the back of the mobile home. And inside the mobile home, ghost images fed to her from the Bug's sensors shift and shuffle, two people's worth of heat signature, with a pulsing homing beacon ping emanating from the head of one of them. She smiles wryly. *Got ya, ya bastard.* "Looks like they're home."

"That was it?" Bernice asks, peeling Finn off her right nipple. He sucks at air for a moment and just as a scream is forming in his mouth, Bernice flips him around to let him latch onto her other breast. "A shitty fence we knocked down by blowing on it, an ice-moat filled with dead alligators, a dozen lousy drones, and a Floyd tribute laser show. Exactly how was that supposed to keep us from finding them, anyway?"

"I think we were supposed to get stoned and maybe freeze to death while we watched the show."

"Guess that would explain the bong and the pile of snack food they left for us. So lame. The whole thing... I mean, they've had a month. Am I wrong to expect a little effort?" Bernice shifts the slowly-waking Jake, his lips puckering, towards her free right nipple.

At the bottom of the hill the Bug slows to a stop, steam whistling out of its leg pistons as the car settles its belly down to the snow in front of the mobile home.

"You're forgetting their inherent laziness," Roxanne says.

"Oh, yeah. Why did we want them back, again?"

"I don't ask that question anymore. The answer always depresses me." Roxanne's nose twitches and her door pops open. "Come on, let's go remind those two idiots just whose men they are."

CHAPTER TWO

"I KNEW I never should have let Rudy build Bernice her own car." Trip stands in the double-wide's doorway, holding the door open for a scowling Roxanne. He gives her a lopsided half-smile, half-smirk around the foot-long cigarette holder clenched in his teeth. The holder doesn't have a cigarette in it.

"Hello to you, too." Roxanne walks up the molded concrete front steps and stops to take in Trip's ratty, faded smoking jacket, the extension cord belt tied tight around his narrow waist, the pink bunny slippers a size too small for his bare size thirteen feet, his unshaven chin, and his unwashed, unkempt hair. She sighs. "Well, on second thought, I probably should be going."

"How'd you find me?" Trip steps back as Roxanne pushes her way past him. "No, wait, let me guess..."

"Tracking pulse from your implant," Roxanne says, unzipping her parka. She rests her hands on her bulging belly. "I put it in when I converted it to wireless. Automatically turns itself on if it's more than a hundred meters from my implant for more than a day."

"Of course it does." Trip watches her hesitantly step into the living room, gingerly looking for clean-ish spots on the floor to put her stiletto-heeled boots. "For the record, I did not run away because you were pregnant," he says, starting to shut the front door. "I merely had to rescue my dear brother from being turned into mush by the pressures of raising twins who are clearly not his own."

Something stops the door from closing. Trip glances back just as Bernice forces her way in, a curly black-haired infant under each arm, sucking madly away at her heavy-with-milk breasts. Trip's eyes linger on her naked boobs.

Bernice snarls at him. "And where is my idiot husband, exactly?" She peers around him into the dark shadows of the cabin.

"In the back playing X-box." Trip snaps the cigarette holder's tip around in his mouth to point down the hallway.

Bernice heads in that direction. "Dear gods, I hope that's not a euphemism."

Roxanne stands in the kitchenette, staring at the sink full of dishes and pots, pans, and outright garbage. "You're living the high life, I see."

Trip stays close to the door, his fingertips brushing the handle. "Haven't had time for the merely physical things. I've been getting to know myself."

"Dear gods I hope that's not a euphemism, either," Roxanne says.

"Not at all. I've taken up meditation. It's so peaceful out here, aside from the roving bands of howler rabbits. Made some startling discoveries."

Roxanne crosses her arms over her chest. "Like how you're an asshole."

"Already established that, I thought. No, I meant new discoveries." Trip taps the nub at the base of his neck, just behind his ear. "About my implant. It's got memory banks, apparently."

"Yeah, saw those when I was in tinkering," Roxanne shrugs. "Wultr bio-bubble memory. So what? We gonna talk about you running off?"

"*So what?* They're not just normal memory banks. They've got memory banks nested within memory banks inside, all hidden away under layers of crypt. I've been deep meditating, really learning how to probe the things. I can feel them there, but I still can't access what's inside."

"How thrilling for you."

"Vishnu's nipples, that's the understatement of the post-apocalypse." Trip edges even closer to the door. "The implant's been passed down generation through generation in my family. The blocked banks could have memories from my mom, or her dad, or his dad, or his aunt... well, you get the idea. And who knows what they thought important enough to lock away?"

"That's awful sentimental of you."

Trip does his crooked half-smile thing. "I'm assuming it's a treasure map or a list of never-fail pick-up lines. You know, something important. Something valuable."

"Ah-hah, there we go."

"Yeah, so, you can see why I have to stick at it. I owe it to future generations to unlock the knowledge."

"Staying here, then?"

Trip nods. "And if you could do me a huge favor and take Rudy with you, it should only take a couple more months of complete isolation. No longer than a year. Maybe five if I have to travel to Tibet to pick up some hard-core meditation techniques from the ubermonks. You know what?" Trip begins to turn the door handle. "I should just head for Tibet now. You know how those ubermonks can get. I'll probably have to fight a succession of acolytes hand-to-hand before they even let me in the Grand Temple." His left eyebrow twitches and outside, the *Wound*'s engine roars on, like some dying bull elephant. "I'll look you and the kid up when I get back, I swear. Ten years, max."

Trip's halfway out the door when the pair of three-inch long needles strike his back and sink right through the smoking jacket and into his shoulder blades. A half second later, 10,000 volts at 600 milliamperes spark down the wires from the stunner Roxanne's pointing at him.

A confused grimace on his long face, Trip convulses and slumps down the concrete block stairs all rag-doll to the hard, frozen ground.

CHAPTER THREE

"SUPPOSE you think that was funny, shooting me."

Trip opens his eyes and stares up at the duct-taped patched roof of the back seat of the *Festering Wound*. He sits up, and there's Roxanne in the passenger seat up front, her stiletto boots up on the driver's seat — his driver's seat. In front of the empty driver's seat the steering wheel makes micro-tracking adjustments, twisting an inch left and a centimeter right at a time. The tip of the antenna behind Roxanne's ear blinks green with each jog of the wheel.

Roxanne glances back at him. "Would explain why I haven't been able to wipe this off my face, yeah," she says, pointing at her mouth, all smiles. "Thinking about making it a regular thing, shooting you."

"No snow." Trip looks out the window and lights a hand-rolled cig. The landscape is bleak, scraggly nuke-polluted scrubland dotted with patches of yellow and brown weeds under a dour, hazy sun. The Wasteland. "How long have I been out?"

Roxanne swings her legs off the driver's seat and faces

forward, gently rubbing her distended stomach. "About a thousand miles. We're almost home."

"A thousand miles?" Trip heaves himself over the back of the front seat and settles in behind the steering wheel. "How did that little stunner of yours keep me out for that long? Its capacitor doesn't even hold enough juice to fricassee a rabbit, and believe me, I've tried."

Roxanne plucks the cig from between Trip's lips and flicks it across his chest and out the open driver's window. "Well, it knocked you flat. After that, I might have kicked you into unconsciousness."

Trip taps the over-ride sequence into the repurposed Sega GameGear jammed haphazardly into a cut-out on the dashboard, the *Wound*'s brain box. The tiny 16-bit screen flashes red, the tip of Rozanne's wireless antenna goes yellow, then out.

The Dodge immediately begins drifting off the lonely stretch of battered 81 North, at ninety miles per.

"You kicked me?" Trip quickly punches in another code. The GameGear screen flashes yellow, and then there in his head is the old familiar presence, the puppy-dog AI of the *Wound*'s brain announcing its reconnection with him, like a big sloppy virtual face licking.

Trip twitches his right eyebrow and the *Wound* swerves back into the middle of the road.

"Well, Bernice helped," Roxanne says. "She's a real artist with a cast-iron skillet."

"Explains this, I guess." Trip touches a pair of fingertips against the welt on the back of his head. He winces while he gingerly probes the massive bump. "Wait a minute... I've been unconscious for the better part of a day. Isn't that, you know, dangerous?"

"Life threatening, even."

"I could have permanent damage, here."

"How would you know?"

"Point."

"So." Roxanne's hand comes to rest on the stun pistol holstered to her hip. "You going to try and run off again?"

"Not if I get naming rights."

"You're not naming our child *The Soulful Jazz Stylings of Groucho Underpants*."

"Not if he's a boy, no."

Up ahead, a cluster of people on foot make their slow way up the road. Trip's eyebrow twitches and the *Wound* jogs to the right, skirting around them. The procession goes on for a half-mile, men and women and children, overstuffed sacks and packs on their backs, wary and hungry expressions on their faces.

"Woah," Trip says, "what's up with all the ped traffic?"

"Refugees." Roxanne touches the platinum double-helix phallus hanging around her neck. *New Gods, I know you probably don't give a shit, nor should you, really, but just in case, watch over us poor bastards*, she mouths in silent prayer.

Trip's eyebrow twitches and the *Wound* speeds up another ten miler per, leaving the procession far behind, covered in the dust kicked up by the car's adaptive tires. "Refugees?"

"Yeah, they've been flooding the Wasteland since the war started. Really stressing the city-states."

"What war?"

"You know very well what war. The war you started before you ran for the hills. You know, between the Chinese and the Cthulists."

"Oh, that one," Trip says with a wry smile. "But I didn't start it. Not technically. I just kinda set circumstances in motion. With extreme and rather clever prejudice, if I do say so myself."

"You started it. And it's turning out to be quite the big one.

The Chinese are trying to occupy the whole continent instead of just the West Coast as the next step in conquering the world, and the Cthulists are trying to forcibly convert us all into squids like them so we won't mind committing ritual suicide to usher in the return of their fictional gods."

"I sense a small amount of concern in your voice, but I wouldn't worry my sexy little head about it, if I were you. For either of them to achieve their goals, they'll have to take the other side out of the picture first. So, with any luck, they'll kill each other off. Problem solved."

"Just hope you're proud of yourself. Refugees have been swarming into the Wasteland for months, now. Every day there's more than the last day. Thousands. And all of them needing food, water, shelter. Stuff the Wasteland isn't exactly overflowing with in the first place." Roxanne's eyes go all thousand-league, a whole-world-on-her-back stare. "We're strained to bursting already, and it's just going to get worse as the war spreads out of the mid-West into the South. Hundreds of thousands more people are going to be displaced, and where are they gonna come? The Wasteland. And it's not just the refugees. The war's eventually going to come here, too. Didn't think about that when you set things in motion, did you?"

"*Au contraire, mon frère.*" Trip fishes a Bugs Bunny Pez dispenser out of his smoking jacket pocket and holds it up to his lips. He bends the head back and pops the last of his home-made stim pellets onto his tongue. "I've got a cunning plan."

"To stop the war?"

"Stop it?" Trip tosses the empty dispenser onto the dash. "Why would I want to stop it? There's too much money to be made."

"Of course. How silly of me."

"Yes, but I still love you." The pellet dissolves almost instantly on Trip's tongue, the special quick-acting blend of iguana urine-laced caffeinated bug spray pretty much instantly banishing the fog of sleeping off a stun-gunning curled up in the back seat of a car. "Granted, the plan got derailed just the tiniest bit when I spontaneously decided to get heavily into meditation and rustic living—"

"You mean when I told you we were pregnant."

Trip leans back, lacing his fingers behind his head, careful to avoid touching the cast-iron inflicted welt. "It may have coincidentally been around that same time, yes."

"Coincidentally? We were lying in bed, I told you we were pregnant, we cuddled for a minute, maybe a minute and a half, then you excused yourself to take a piss. And poof, you never came back."

"You wouldn't think to look at it, but the outhouse at the trailer, you will never take a more comfortable piss. Anyway, this couldn't have worked out better for us. With all these refugees I'll have my pick of good, cheap, desperate labor. And an exploitable workforce is one of the cornerstones of a profitable business."

"What do you need a workforce for?"

"Two words: Mechwarbots."

"That's one word," Roxanne says. "Haven't you learned your lesson where warbots are concerned? The last batch you made turned tail and ran for the hills the second a simple unarmed angry mob came knocking at the city wall."

"That was a bug in their limited AI systems."

"Seeding them with your personality and your inherent predilection for fleeing at the first sign of responsibility was a bug?"

"The new 2.0 Mechwarbots, they'll be dumbed-down task-specific combat and defense expert system models. They'll take orders, execute them, all without personality—mine or anybody else's. And they'll be pretty straightforward to manufacture. I figure with a good assembly line and enough cheap marginally skilled labor we'll be able to churn out two, maybe three bots a day once we're fully ramped up."

"Ambitious."

"Oh, I know what you're thinking, but you said it yourself, this war is just gonna get bigger and bigger. There will be plenty of buyers."

"Yay?" Roxanne asks without enthusiasm.

"Hey, don't worry. I'll give a special two-percent Wasteland discount to the city-states, and as Shunk's Minister of Defense and Morale, I think I can confidently state Shunk will be buying the first batch off the assembly line—"

"It's not going to be that easy."

"I know, I know. Your dad has final say on all capital expenditures, but let's be real, all I need to do is get Morty slightly more drunk than he normally is and he'll sign anything I put in front of him."

"Look, Trip, there have been some changes while you were gone. We should probably talk about them before we get back—"

"Yeah, sure, let's talk." Trip puts his hand on Roxanne's thigh. "But first, it has been a while. And unlike my brother, I'm not a chronic masturbator. So I got a lot of juices backed up."

"What, now?"

Trip jogs his head at the back seat and wags his eyebrows. "Car can drive itself."

"Well, what you waiting for?" she asks, pulling off her boots. "Go on, hop on back."

CHAPTER FOUR

LEANED BACK on the salvaged 1983 Impala back seat that serves as Rudy's front room couch, Trip swings his Converses up on the cinder-block and wood plank coffee table. "So, how was it? Comfy?"

"What are you talking about?" Rudy comes through the tattered Empire Strikes Back bedsheet hanging in the doorway to the back room, zipping up his stomach. Shirtless, his chest hair is matted with sweat and his usual five-o'clock shadow looks more like ten PM shadow, practically a full beard. The circles under his eyes are dark and puffy. "How was what?"

"The doghouse. I'm just presuming that's where Bernie had you sleeping last night."

Eyes bloodshot and bleary, Rudy grabs a T-shirt from the waist-high pile of clothes in the corner of the room and shrugs into it without bothering to turn it right-side out. "I did not sleep in the doghouse."

"It's because you don't have a doghouse, isn't it? I keep telling you, you need a dog." Trip pulls a rusty cough drop tin out from one of the dozens of pockets sewn into the lining of his tux jacket. He cracks it open and plucks one of the hand rolled cigs out. For this batch, he'd used a newspaper bartered from a landfill-turned-supply-post outside of Montoursville as paper. The fragment of story on the cig tells of a rash of genetically-modified cornstalks menacing Harrisburg in the aftermath of the third meltdown at Three-Mile Island, a hundred and fifty years ago. Trip pops the cig between his lips and fishes a big Zippo out of another pocket. "Then you could sleep in its house instead of the couch," he says, lighting the cig.

Rudy glares at the cig. "You can't smoke in here."

"*You* can't smoke in here," Trip says, slipping the lighter away.

Rudy looks around for something, his nose twitching. He idly twists his left nipple through the T-shirt to prime the pump of his internal pharma factory. His stomach lets out a sputtering whine as the factory comes online, pumping calming THC analog directly into his bloodstream as fast as the implant can make it. "That coffee I smell? Please say you made coffee."

"I made coffee." Trip nods his head at the Franklin stove in the center of the room and the twelve-cup percolator sitting on top of it. "But it's a small pot, so I don't think there's going to be any left for you, to be honest. So you slept in the Bug, then. Same difference."

Rudy grabs a random half-empty mug from the collection of dozens on the folding card/dining room table, dumps whatever it is that's in it down his throat, and pads over to the stove, his bare feet pushing baby toys and stuffed animals out of the way. "My house, my coffee." He fills the mug, hands that to Trip, then takes the percolator with him as he plops down in a chair, the driver's seat from a 1999 Mazda Miata. "And, I wish I'd slept in the Bug," he says, slugging down coffee straight from the percolator. "Bernie slept in the Bug."

Bernice slips sideways through the Empire sheet, a sleeping baby in each arm. "And super glad I did. First full night's sleep I've had in months." She steps in front of Rudy. "Okay, here you go. — Little help here, Trip?"

Trip puts his mug down on the coffee table, and leans over, prying the percolator away from Rudy. Rudy's hands now free, Bernice lays Finn in Rudy's lap, then puts Jake down next to his brother on Rudy's knee.

Rudy looks down at his sons. Finn's eyes flutter like he is about to wake up. And start crying. "What am I supposed to do with these?"

Bernice purses her lips. "Be a dad."

"I was a dad last night," Rudy says, rocking Finn. The baby's eyes stop fluttering, crying wake-up averted. "Today I was hoping to catch up on the sleep I missed being that dad."

"Maybe you should have thought of that before you let this idiot here drag you to Florida." Bernice adjusts the leather corset of her Sisters of No-Mercy uniform, shifting her breasts to stress her cleavage as proscribed by Holy Edict. "Now, I gotta go. Sergeant-at-Arm's business to attend to. I should be back by dinner. I'm expecting steaks. And cow this time. I'll know if you try to pass off mutant cockroach again."

"Do we have any cow?" Rudy asks.

Bernice grins. "We don't have *anything*. I left the grocery list on the ice chest." She bends over Rudy, kissing each baby on the forehead, then pecks Rudy on the cheek. "Laters," she says, and she's gone out the front door.

Trip smirks after her. "Have I mentioned I am so glad you married her?"

"I did kind of leave her in the lurch," Rudy says. "And the boys... I should never have left them. Should have never have let you talk me into going in the first place. Damn fool idea."

Trip shrugs, picking up his mug and blowing into it. "Speaking of damn fool ideas, time we got the 'bot factory up and running again."

"What factory? It's a corner in a warehouse where we pieced together a dozen warbots out of junkyard spare parts."

Trip takes a sip of the coffee. "And after you build us a proper assembly line, it'll be a factory."

"While I'm building the assembly line, what will you be doing?"

"What else? Drumming up business and making deals. And meditating. Mostly meditating." Trip knocks a knuckle against the side of his head. "I gotta find out what's locked in here. So, we going or what?"

"Yeah, hold on," Rudy says, shifting the babies around in his arms and standing, moving slow to try to keep them asleep as long as possible. "Just let me get the stroller."

"Do we have to take them with us?"

"You are gonna make such a great dad."

CHAPTER FIVE

"WHAT THE HELL IS THIS, SHEMP?"

At the warehouse on the southern side of the walled city-state of Shunk, Trip strides through the open loading bay and up to the tall man with the Mohawk standing with a clipboard in front of stacked barrels of beer.

Shemp glances up from his clipboard. "What is what, Trip?" he asks, making a check on an inventory control form with a nub of a pencil.

Trip waves his hands out at the stacks, stretching deep into the warehouse, barrels five high to the ceiling in some places. Workers move in and out of the stacks pulling low-slung wheeled carts, some bringing more, some taking barrels away. "All that."

"Beer." Shemp looks lovingly at the stacks. "As far as the eye can see. Isn't it wonderful?"

"Yeah, sure, wonderful," Trip says with a sneer. "But what's it doing in my factory?"

Shemp lowers his clipboard and slips the nub of a pencil away behind his left ear. "*Your* factory?"

"Robot factory, yeah. Says so right on the door. Or it was supposed to. I put it on Rudy's to-do list to get a logo painted, but you know how lazy that bastard is. Seriously, how hard is it to get through a four-thousand item to-do list, I ask you?"

"You haven't been around for months. We thought you'd abandoned it." Shemp waves over Trip's shoulder. "Hey there, Rudy!"

Rudy stands framed in the open loading bay door, standing on the ramp behind a twin-pod wicker pram with mismatched wheels, adjusting the complex feeding armature over the left pod so that little, crying Jake can reach the suspended bottle. Rudy waves back at Shemp absently, then returns to adjusting.

"I did," Trip says. "But I'm getting the band back together."

"Sorry, dude," Shemp says. "Need the space."

"For what?"

"Um, the beer."

"For the beer?"

"Yeah, for the beer. We've about run out of places to make it, let alone store it. Shit, I'm storing fifty barrels at my house. You got any room at your place for a couple dozen barrels?"

"No. When did this happen?"

"It's the war, dude. Demand's gone through the roof, from both sides. You know what they say, armies run on booze—courage for the troops, and fuel for the tanks. Not to mention all the refugees. All they've got is sorrows to drown. We're producing four times what we were before the war, and more every day. Pretty soon we're going to have to start importing wheat—we can't grow the stuff fast enough ourselves, especially now that the refugee camps are encroaching on what little farmland we have."

"Yeah, that's great. Rah-rah for the local economy—and you're welcome, by the way." Trip pauses to light a cig. "Okay, so, you're using this place. Where's my new place?"

"New place?" Shemp asks.

"Yeah. You did find me a new place to set up shop, didn't you?"

"Was I supposed to?"

"Vishnu's nipples. *Was he supposed to?* Of course you were supposed to. It's just common courtesy."

Shemp rubs the back of his neck. "Oh, sorry... I didn't—"

"Don't worry about it, it's not too late to make things right." Trip thumps Shemp on the shoulder with an open palm. "Now, two-o'clock this afternoon, *that* would be too late. Okay, tell you what. I'm not an unreasonable guy, and I was gonna have a long lunch, anyway. So you've got until, let's say two-thirty."

"To find you a place to set up shop?"

"Yep. With enough space for an auto-lathe, polymer injection molder, 3D-printer, laser die-cutter, computer-controlled quality assurance testing rig, Cerebro Mark Two, and 1:1 scale model of the Millennium Vulcan, be-sainted patron of giant-headed cultural icons."

"Do you have any of that stuff?" Shemp asks.

"No, but I have a robot who can slowly build other robots by hand. That's a start. The rest we'll import from So-Cali. Assuming my credit's still good with the Chinese... yeah, probably shouldn't count on that. You know anybody with good credit we can use as a front?" Trip scans the warehouse. "Speaking of my robot, where is Hunt-R, anyway? I distinctly remember telling that over-rated clockwork to guard this place while I was gone. A job he's done about as spectacularly as I assumed he would. He is so not getting that second eye he wanted for National Consumerism Day."

"You mean that robot of yours? He high-tailed it right after we moved in. He said the beer was keeping him up at night. I see him hanging out in the square every now and then."

"Okay, well, I'm gonna go get him, publicly dress him down

for dereliction of duty, and have lunch." Trip raises an eyebrow and smirks at Shemp. "And you will be?"

"Finding you a place to set up shop?"

"Finding me a place to set up shop, yep, that's a good man."

"I'd love to help you out, Trip—I feel bad about taking this place over, I do, but it ain't gonna happen." Shemp pauses while a whistle from the adjoining loading bay announces the arrival of an oxen-drawn truck ready for loading. "Look, I've gotta go," he says, and walks off.

"Oh, I see, right." Trip follows him. "I thought you and me were beyond that sort of thing, Shemp, but if that's the way you want this to go, we can let blatant greed and corruption deal a death blow to our burgeoning friendship. So how much is this going to cost me?"

Shemp stops and turns around. "I'm not looking for cash, Trip, I'm really not. Even if there was any place in Shunk left for non-beer manufacturing, I couldn't get it for you. The Sorta Council nationalized everything in the name of beer production once they realized we were heading into the biggest beer boom-time the Wasteland's seen since the Kochite-Murdockian war of '76. They've got first and final say on that sort of thing now." He shrugs apologetically. "It's out of my hands."

CHAPTER SIX

"ALMS, ALMS FOR A POOR BLIND ROBOT?"

Hunt-R sits on the ground at the base of the junk-parts fountain in Shunk's town square, nestled between a booth selling fried cockroach balls and a much busier one selling beer, waving a rusty soup can in front of him at the people standing in line.

"Since when are you blind?"

The robot pushes the dirty rag up off his single large, unlit eye. "Since it makes good business," Hunt-R says, the yellow light in his eye snapping on. The robot tilts its flat face up at Trip, smirking down on him, then over at Rudy and his progeny in their pram. *Oh, look, idiots* and *crying babies. Better off ignoring the lot of them.* Hunt-R shuts his eye off and waves the can in front of him again. "Alms, alms for a poor, blind robot?"

"What's an alm, anyway?" Rudy asks. "Anybody actually know?"

"Isn't it a tree?" Trip asks. "I'm pretty sure it's a tree. Which begs the question, what does a robot need with trees? Okay, maybe one tree, but any more than that, they're just going to get underfoot."

"I think you're thinking of Oak trees," Rudy says, twisting his nipple through his inside-out T-shirt.

Trip nods. "Right. Always get those two confused."

"Is this how it's going to be until I acknowledge you?" Hunt-R turns his eye back on. "Idiot banter while you block potential suckers from being charitable?"

Trip lights a cigarette and smirks at Rudy. "Don't know about you, but I do feel a lot of pent-up idiot banter in me wanting out."

"Yeah, I could banter all day," Rudy says, gently shoving pacifiers into both baby's mouth simultaneously, quieting them. "All night, even. Lack of sleep brings out the banter in me."

Hunt-R lowers the can. "All right, all right, let's get this over with. It's lunchtime. I'm losing prime begging time. Can't you just leave me be? What do you want with me now?"

"What do you think we want?" Trip asks. "We're getting into the military-industrial complex business. Gonna be building some honking big wheeled war machines. Congratulations, you're employee number three. If we intended to pay you, you'd get stock options. But since we already own your sorry metallic ass, get it moving and come on." Trip spins on his heel and starts to walk off, clearly expecting to be followed.

"Wait, what's that about wheeled war machines?" Rudy stays put, retrieving Finn's red-and-blue polka-dotted blankey from the end of the pram where it's been kicked by flailing baby feet. He gives the blankey to the grasping baby, who draws it tight, immediately spitting out his pacifier in favor of sucking a corner of fabric. "I thought we were going to build warbots."

Trip spins around on his heel and comes back, blowing smoke out of his nostrils. "I'm sorta off robots."

"Since when?" Rudy asks.

"Since... that." Trip points his cig down at Hunt-R. "You can't say he's anything other than an embarrassment. Out here making a spectacle of himself like this. It's shameful, really, to see how far he's fallen. If he was my kid, I'd disown him."

"I'll have you know I clear over four hundred a day doing this," Hunt-R says, rattling the cup. "Enough for a two-bedroom uptown."

Trip spreads his arms wide. "Son!"

"Stuff it, *dad*. Look, I'm not interested in another of your hare-brained schemes, robots or wheeled war machines or whatever it is. So, if you're not in the charitable mood—which I doubt at least you ever are, Programmer Trip—then please stand aside. It's lunchtime. Prime begging hours."

"Okay, okay." Trip takes a small black box out of a jacket-lining pocket. "Oh, look, what do we have here?" He runs his thumb lightly over the big red button. "A remote control with a button. I wonder what brain it resets to Day One, erasing all those precious memories built up over the years and returning the ungrateful robot to the sassless, free-will free servant he used to be? Shall we find out?"

"You're such a dick." A panel pops open in Hunt-R's chest and the robot shoves the can inside. "So, we're in the *warcars* business now, then?"

"Megacar business, I think. Better branding." Trip dashes his cig out on the top of Hunt-R's head. "Anyway, I think somebody else already owns the warcar trademark. Startup's gonna have enough problems without having to worry about that kinda fight, too. Besides, trademark attorneys are the worst. All right, let's go throw my considerable political weight around and brow-beat Morty until he gives us a warehouse, rent-free. And free labor. You know, for our trouble."

"You think it's gonna be that easy?" Rudy asks.

Trip laces his fingers together and cracks his knuckles with a smug grin. "I'm practically his son-in-law. The old coot will do anything for me."

"Doesn't hurt that he's usually drunk off his ass," Hunt-R notes.

Trip lights another cig. "That too."

"So," Rudy asks Hunt-R, "what you think of the rig?"

"The pram?"

Rudy nods. "Independent suspension. Cup holders. Hands-free feeding system. And plenty of storage in the bottom. For, like, sundries."

Why do I suddenly feel very, very apprehensive? Hunt-R asks himself. "It's very nice, I suppose."

"Glad you like it. It's yours."

Ah, that's why. "I don't need a pram," Hunt-R says.

"Trust me, it's easier than carrying them around in your arms."

"Carrying who around?"

"Who do you think?" Rudy shoves the pram forward with his boot. "Job one. Look after them."

"Oh, no." Hunt-R stands, his under-lubricated joints creaking, his actuating servos whirring loudly. He pushes the pram back towards Rudy with his knee. "That's a step too far. I'm not babysitting your brood."

"You were built to do our dirty work," Trip reminds him.

"That's too dirty," Hunt-R says. "Shit comes out of them. Often. And they're very loud."

"Don't I know it," Rudy says. "Good thing you can turn off your scent and hearing gear."

"Why are we even having this discussion?" Trip asks. "You're gonna do it, robot."

"No, I'm putting my foot down," Hunt-R says, putting his fists on his hips with a defiant *clang*. "I'm an incredibly advanced piece of technology, not some undertrained slab of alloy to be vomited on."

"Don't think of it as babysitting." Trip drapes his arm around the robot's shoulders in feigned camaraderie. "Think of it as an opportunity to turn the little rug-rats against their own dad."

"Or uncle," Rudy says.

"Nah, they'd never turn against me. Admire me. Aspire to be me. Bask in my glow, sure. But never turn against me." Trip bends down to pinch a rosy, blanket-sucking cheek. "Right, little Jake?"

"That's Finn," both Rudy and Hunt-R say.

Trip shrugs. "Does it matter?" he asked, walking off.

"You hear that?" Rudy asks Hunt-R. "With him as an uncle they're going to need all the help they can get to avoid turning into psychopaths. Come on. Please."

Hunt-R pulls the tram closer. "I'm not changing their diapers. I do have my principles."

"You will," Rudy says.

"Oh, I will, will I? What makes you think that?"

"It's good karma."

"Karma is bullshit."

"Probably, yeah. So, how about this for a reason, then: Trip's not the only one with a reset button."

"Should I use disposables or cloth?"

—

CHAPTER SEVEN

"I'M SORRY, sir, I can't let you in," the tall, twenty-something brunette in the skin covering but curve accentuating armor-plated leather jumpsuit tells Trip with a firm hand pressed against his chest as he tries to push past her while reaching for Morty's front door. "The Sorta Council is in session."

Trip takes hold of the brunette's wrist and gently pulls her hand away from his chest. "Which is exactly why you can let me in."

"Sorry, sir," the brunette says, her hand dropping down to her side to rest not-at-all-casually on the duct-taped handle of a sawed-off shotgun hanging in a quick-draw holster on her thigh. "Please move along."

"I haven't been out of town that long," Trip says, a whine of indignation cracking his voice. "How do you not know who I am? I'm the Minister of War."

"She's a new recruit, sir," the younger, shorter blonde standing on the other side of the doorway says. "He's the Mother Superior's old man, Sharon."

"A new recruit to what?" Trip asks the blonde. She's wearing the same get-up as the brunette, only with a pillbox hat, silver epaulets on her shoulders, and a rusty four-shot .50 revolver on her thigh.

"Sisters of No-Mercy, *doy*," the brunette says with a roll of her eyes.

"Hey, watch the attitude, missy," the blonde snaps at the brunette.

The brunette lowers her head sheepishly. "Sorry, Lieutenant."

Trip wags a finger at the women. "Those are not Sisters of No-Mercy outfits. Not enough cleavage, and not a hint of fishnet. You gotta have fishnet."

"They're our civil patrol uniforms," the blonde says, unzipping the jumpsuit at the collar just low enough so she can pull out the small bronze intertwined phalluses that hang around her neck on a braided leather necklace to show Trip. "They're designed to be functional, non-threatening, and authoritative, yet still expressing our womanly souls."

Trip frowns at the Sister's holy symbol as the blonde tucks it away and zips back up. "Since when do the Sisters of No-Mercy have a civil patrol?"

"Not all the new refugees Shunk's hosting play nice with others," the blonde says. "Somebody had to step up to be a police force, and us Sisters, we're all about public service. The Mother Superior saw a need, and filled it."

"Just like the militia unit Sister Gwendolyn is putting together from the refugee recruits to act as a home defense force," Rudy says, lighting a cig as he steps up next to Trip.

"Militia?" Trip asks, yanking the cig away from Rudy for himself. "Civil patrol?"

Rudy nods. "You didn't know?"

"You did?"

"Bernie told me."

"About the militia and the civil patrol?"

"About everything. —We do talk, me and the wife. Rox hasn't brought up any of this with you?"

Trip snorts. "We've been busy. You know, with make-up schtupping."

"So you don't know?" Rudy smiles. Big and unabashed. "Oh, this is gonna be good."

"What's that supposed to mean?" Trip asks.

"You'll see." Rudy turns to the blonde. "Can you let us in, Dorris? We do have business for the council. Plus, I really want to see this."

"Ooh," Hunt-R calls out from a little ways up the dirt lane where he's adjusting the feeding armatures on the twins' pram. "Take pictures!"

CHAPTER EIGHT

"WHERE'S MORTY?" Trip asks, scanning the dark living room where Shunk's ruling Sorta council sits in session in folding chairs around three card tables pushed together.

At least they saved a space for me, Trip thinks, spotting the empty chair at the other end of the tables. He heads for it, reaching over the scuba-gear wearing Minister of Sewage's shoulder as he passes to dash his cig out in an ashtray.

"Right here, Trip," says some clean-shaved, slick-backed hair, pinstripe bathrobe-wearing Korean guy at the head of the tables Trip doesn't know, and who, unlike everybody else, suspiciously doesn't have a mug of beer in front of them.

"Yeah, right," Trip says, plopping down in the empty chair. He smirks across the tables at the guy. "Morty's all scruffy and has a lisp. You can't be Morty – you don't even reek of booze." Trip takes a cig and his Zippo out while he glances around him. "Seriously, where is he? There are apologies to be made. To me, by him, it really should go without saying."

"Seriously, Trip," the guy says. "It's me."

"Morty?" Trip pauses, the flame of the lighter an inch from the tip of the cig in his lips, and squints, finally taking note of the guy's eyes: one cloudy and looking straight and steady at him, the other clear and bright, and staring up at the ceiling. "What the hell happened?"

"I gave up drinking."

"You?" Trip huffs, lighting the cig and snapping the Zippo closed. "Gave up drinking?"

"Had to, as a matter of civic duty." Morty picks up a glass of water from in front of him and gives it a tentative sip, with a wince, as if he's not quite used to the lack of bite but resigned to it anyway. "Being drunk all the time was fine when Shunk was a hole-in-the-wall, but that's changed. Our population's quintupled since the war started up — that's a lot of people, and a lot more administration. More decisions to be made, important decisions. Housing, utilities, beer production and logistics. Shunk needs me to be sober."

"And I need you to explain why the Sorta council is meeting without their Minister of War." Trip leans back and throws his feet up on the card table. "Did nobody tell you I was back in town?"

"Oh, I told them," Roxanne says, emerging from the doorway to the kitchen. "Sorry about the constant bathroom breaks, folks. Now, where were we?"

"You were detailing the new defense plan," Minister of Sewage Hattie says, his voice muffled by the snorkel bit in his mouth.

"New defense plan?" Trip's left eyebrow goes up. "When did I come up with a new defense plan? And why don't I remember coming up with a new defense plan?"

Roxanne steps up behind Trip and puts her hands on his shoulders. "Okay, Trip, try not to get upset."

"Upset? Why would I get upset? Just losing my memory, is all. Next thing you know I'll be putting on weight and walking around town in a kimono, pining for the old days and looking for teenagers to shoot for not getting off my lawn."

"You're not losing your memory," Roxanne says.

"Oh, you'd better hope I'm losing my memory, because if I'm not, that means someone else is daring to make defense plans." Trip leans forward, shrugging his shoulders out from under Roxanne's hands and glaring at Morty. "And that will not stand. Defense plans, war plans, and picking out the dessert items for the Winter Solstice party—that's all squarely the purview of the Minister of War."

"You didn't tell him?" Morty asks, his cloudy eye darting to look at his daughter.

"I've been busy," Roxanne says.

"Right," Morty says with a sigh. "Trip, Roxanne *is* our Minister of War. And Defense."

"Aha!" Trip exclaims. "I knew it—you didn't give up booze."

"I did," Morty says. "And she is our new minister."

Trip purses his lips and stares at the glowing end of his cig. "I am literally speechless."

"Except you just spoke," Rudy says from where he stands, arms folded across his chest, against the back of the closed front door. "So, not literally."

Trip jabs a finger in Rudy's direction. "I swear to Shatner if you don't wipe that idiot grin off your face I'm going to—"

"To what?" Rudy says, his grin getting bigger. "Sick your army on me? Oh, wait, you don't command an army anymore."

"I'll deal with you later," Trip barks, then sits back and gathers himself. After an indulgent moment of tight-lipped seething, he looks at Morty. "Please, do explain."

Morty takes another sip of water. "You were gone, Trip, and

with the war refugees flooding us, we had to have someone here who could coordinate and manage keeping Shunk safe and civil."

"Well, I'm back now."

"The thing is, son, Roxanne's been doing a helluva job." Morty smiles warmly at Roxanne. "Even with all these new people, crime's actually down. And the city's better defended than it's ever been."

"Yeah," Hattie says around his snorkel mouthpiece. "It's nice to have a city guard that doesn't run off at the first sign of trouble."

"That's a dig at my robots, isn't it?" Trip scowls at the Minister of Sewage, with his ridiculous shock of white hair and tattered scuba wet suit. "You really want to start something with me, fat boy?"

"It's a glandular condition," Hattie says. He reaches across his massive stomach for the sawed-off speargun strapped to his thigh. "And I'd be more than happy to discuss it further with you. Outside. At thirty paces. Below the surface."

"Settle down, you two, nobody's dueling." Morty waves his hands before him, calling for calm. "The point is, Trip, we've all talked it over, and we're sticking with Roxanne. If she'll stick with us."

"Sorry, hon," Roxanne says, shooing Trip out of her chair. "How about I make it up to you tonight? Nice cozy romantic evening, just you and me." She rubs her bulging belly. "And the player to be named later, of course."

Trip stands, brushing imaginary dust off the lapels of his tux and shrugging with sudden, obviously feigned nonchalance. "Yeah, well, I never wanted to be Minister of War, anyway."

"Excellent," Morty says, clapping his hands and rubbing them together. "Now that that's all settled... if you'll excuse us, son, there's pressing business to attend to."

"No excuses necessary," Trip says. "That's why I'm here. Pressing business. I need my warehouse back."

"Your warehouse?" Morty asks.

"Yeah, the one that's currently, and quite annoyingly, being used to store that vile piss water you call beer."

"Piss water or not, it's making us literal shit-loads of money," Morty says. "And we need every bit of warehouse space inside the walls as we can get."

"So you're telling me beer is more important to you than the livelihood of your daughter's baby daddy?"

"It's more complicated than that, Trip," Morty says. "The beer pays the bills. It's what's paying for the new sewage system. And that will benefit everyone. So even if better sanitation was the only thing to consider, yes, I'd have to go with the beer if it means never again having to deal with shit overflowing onto the streets every time it rains."

"Here, here," Hattie says.

"Does it have to be a warehouse?" Roxanne asks, settling herself down into the chair slowly.

"Just someplace with walls and a roof where we can build war cars," Rudy answers.

"How about a field where you can build war cars after you build some walls and roof?" asks Davenport, the Minister of Food and Stuff. "And I should mention it's outside the city walls, if that's a problem."

"What are you thinking?" Morty asks.

The blue-haired Davenport pushes her glasses up her crooked nose. "That patch of field on the other end of the refugee camp."

"The old industrial waste dump?" Roxanne asks.

Davenport nods. "It's no good for growing grain, and it'd be unsafe for anyone to live there, but, as long as you avoid the chemicals that bubble out of the ground when it's above 60 degrees, and don't dig your foundation deeper than the foot of topsoil, it might be perfect for your little war car business."

Trip sneers. "A dump? Might work if it was only someplace for Rudy to crash, but I'll be working there. Occasionally. When I don't have something better to do–"

"We'll take it," Rudy interrupts.

"Fine." Trip snorts. "But only until the beer economy crashes and we can get our old warehouse back."

"Good, then it's settled," Morty says. "We'll work out the details of rent later."

"Rent?" Trip's cig drops from his mouth. "What rent? We never paid rent before."

Morty shrugs apologetically. "Well, that was when you were a minister."

CHAPTER NINE

"DO you believe the nerve of that guy?" Trip asks, striding out the front door of Morty's house. "Rent. From me. It is both unprecedented and alarming."

"I've never seen you out-negotiated before," Rudy says, stepping out into the street after Trip. He glances around for Hunt-R. The robot, and his kids, are nowhere to be seen. He shrugs and gives his nipple a soft tweak. "I think I've got a new hero."

"I took it easy on him," Trip says out of the corner of his mouth as he lights a cig and heads north up the dirt and loose stone excuse for a main street. "You know, 'cause he's old and frail."

Rudy follows his brother. "If anybody took anybody, it was him taking you. Like out to the wood shed and spanking you with a coffee table while a dwarf in a Richard Nixon costume plays the bongos in the corner."

Trip's left eyebrow goes up. "A dwarf in a Richard Nixon costume?"

"Yeah, and the bongos are skinned with the ass-cheek flesh of Spiro Agnew."

"That's some unusual imagery, even for you."

"New THC analog mix." Rudy pats his stomach and smiles dreamily. "Added in some LSD. For flavor."

Trip stops short to avoid tripping over a dog-sized rat darting in front of him from the alley. He stays stopped to wait for the pair of machete-wielding, dirty-faced pre-teens chasing the rat to pass. "Ah."

"Yeah," Rudy says as the two start walking again. "Anyway, who knew Morty had it in him?"

"He used to be quite the ball breaker CFO, according to Rox, before the big crash of '207 and the siren call of beer brought him to the Wasteland. But let's make one thing perfectly clear, here. I did not get taken. Morty and this piss-ant town of his is what's getting taken, here."

"Sure, we're just paying more per month on a patch of unde-veloped industrial wasteland than we paid for a year's worth of rent at the place in Cali, and that was an actual building."

"As usual, you're not seeing the forest for the killer mutant oaks. You're forgetting the refugee influx."

"Don't know how I could." Rudy thumbs back over his shoulder in the approximate direction of the center of town. "You know how much they wanted for rat-on-a-stick in the square this morning? Twice what they wanted yesterday, and that was three times what they wanted a week before that. Inflation's going through the roof."

Trip punches the air with his cig. "Exactly. All these refugees flooding in, ruining the economy... What do you think they're doing with their time?"

"Started a Ska band that roams around the back country in a psychedelically painted van solving mysteries with a talking dog?"

"Just how much LSD did you mix in?"

"Only forty-seven percent. I haven't had any in ages, figured I'd start low."

"Very wise," Trip says as they pass a corrugated-steel and cardboard shack of a home that's been converted into a recruiting center for the Sisters of No Mercy's civil patrol. There's a line of girls out the door, a couple dozen long. Trip winces and stamps his cig out on the street in front of it before walking on, heading straight for Shunk's main gate at the end of the street. "Anyway, all those refugees, they're just standing around, picking their noses and asses, bored and unemployed, waiting for some handsome cyborg industrialist to come along and give their lives purpose."

"Egomaniacal leanings aside, I have to admit that's pretty noble."

"Noble as shit, damn straight. Can you say *dirt cheap labor pool?*"

"And there's the brother I know."

"It's the perfect buyer's market. We're gonna cover the cost of the rent and more by hiring refugees for next to nothing," Trip says as they pass under the open arch in the city-state's wall of stacked flattened cars out into Shunk's new suburbs, a vast, loose sea of tents and cardboard lean-to's, swarming with hundreds if not thousands of refugees. "Profit margin maintained. Morty taken. Trip triumphant, as if there was ever any doubt."

"So, let me see if I've got this straight," Rudy says. "This plan of yours depends on a large number of unemployed, bored people willing to work for you for next to nothing."

"Willing and thrilled to do so," Trip says, giving Rudy a confident half-smile. "We'll be hailed as heroes, the only guys in this damn town willing to step up and give the schlubs a reason to keep on living."

Rudy frowns. "Not the only guys, though," he says, tipping his head at a patch of tent-free ground up ahead where dozens of booths and tables have been set up.

"Wait... what?" Trip asks, slowing to a stop. He scans the booths. Each and every one is advertising some kind of employment opportunity. Jobs at the brewery. Jobs at the beer warehouses. Jobs trucking beer. Jobs guarding beer. Jobs procuring grain, for beer. Along with the jobs themselves, the placards nailed to the booths and the hawkers manning the booths shout about competitive salaries, paid vacations and holidays, and employer-provided daycare — and of course, free beer just for talking to a representative. "Vishnu's overdue parking tickets, what the Shatner is this?"

"Job fair, looks like."

Trip nods slowly. "Job fair," he says through pursed lips.

"Pretty big one, too. You know, I don't think we're gonna get schlubs for cheap," Rudy says, noting the surprisingly thin crowd of refugees strolling through the area, idly checking out the booths, sipping beers, not looking desperate for work at all.

"Son. Of. A. Bitch."

"Yep," Rudy says. "Is it the LSD or are they actually fighting over the refugees?" he asks as a shouting match breaks out between hawkers from two neighboring booths over a passing refugee.

"No, I see it, too."

"Even the giant inflatable swords?"

"No, those are the LSD."

"So, not a buyer's market, then?"

"Nope," Trip says, lighting a cig. "Quite the opposite."

"Sellers market."

"Yep."

Rudy pats Trip on the back. "Quite the triumph you've got yourself, here, dude."

"Don't suppose I can convince you to jump into the fray?"

Trip asks as a fist is swung and the shouting match becomes a full-on brawl, other hawkers throwing themselves into the fray, the fought-over refugee shrugging and walking on. "You know maybe snag us a couple employees through brute, drug-induced force?"

Rudy shakes his head. "No way am I getting anywhere near those chocolate dinosaurs."

"Chocolate dinosaurs?"

"Both delicious and ferocious. —So what's the plan now?"

"We need workers." Trip spins on his heel and starts walking back to the main gate. "Dirt cheap workers."

Rudy follows, glancing back cautiously at the dinosaurs, their skin melting in the heat of the day, rivulets of gooey brown sloshing onto the rippling, cotton-candy ground. "We ain't gonna find them here."

"Nope, there's blood in the water, and the sharks can smell it. We can't afford to pay a tenth what these guys are offering."

"You know... there is one place where there might just be a good pool of dirt cheap workers. Just down the road. For the asking."

"Problem is who I'd have to ask."

"Sure, she was going to kill Roxanne, but technically she is family," Rudy says as they walk under the arch. "We forgive family. Well, most family."

"Oh, yeah, right... forgot she did that."

"You think she's gonna want to have a say in the war car design, don't you?"

Trip nods. "I swear, she tries to fuck with the software, I'll EMP that egomaniacal nanotech pseudo-daughter of mine into a puddle."

"So, when you wanna leave? Sooner the better." Rudy lowers his voice and jogs his head at one of the stacks of beer barrels flanking the open door to yet another new building, the Shunk

Welcome and Bulk Beer Ordering Center just inside the main gate. "I do not like the way that peanut-butter filled tyrannosaurus over there is eyeing me."

"Can't. Tonight I have to let Rox try and mend the fence she drove the truck carrying the Ministry of War she stole out from under me through." Trip sighs. "Should be fun."

CHAPTER TEN

THERE ARE rose petals on the floor. Okay, not rose petals — the Wasteland doesn't do roses. So what if they're just torn pieces of newspaper? There are hundreds of them, so many they're practically ankle deep. And dozens of candles on the equipment racks lining the walls, casting flickering warm yellow light. And a generous cheese and cracker plate. And a tray of assorted body oils.

And Trip lying there on the Queen-sized mattress in the middle of the floor, all naked except for the sheet demurely covering his knees.

Roxanne walks into the bedroom, lost in her own thoughts, and leans against the door sill, sliding her boots off.

Trip clears his throat and she looks up, finally seeing him there.

A bemused smile spreads across her face. "What's all this?"

"Hmm, let me see." Trip lazily rolls onto his side and props his head up on his fist. "We've got candles, oils, and post-coital snacks... I'm just guessing, but I'd say it might be someone's expecting sex."

"Oh, yeah, right." Roxanne shrugs out of her minister's jacket and hangs it on a wall hook. "Romantic evening."

"Incredibly romantic," Trip says. "Down right impossible to resist romantic. Which is why I'm just a little confused that you're not completely naked already. The jacket's a start, but if that pantsuit isn't off in the next ten seconds, I'm going to feel really bad about making Hunt-R shred all these newspapers. Not to mention putting him through all that trouble to track down cheese that wasn't made from rad-rat milk."

"We might have a problem."

"Zipper on that pantsuit stuck?" Trip waggles his fingers at her. "Come here and I'll fix that right quick."

"It's not the zipper," Roxanne says, drawing the zipper down all the way from under her left armpit to her left ankle. "It's the schedule."

"The schedule?" Trip asks, sitting up. "What schedule?"

"My schedule." Roxanne lets the pantsuit drop to the floor. She stands there naked but for the heavy golden chain and double-helix phallus of her office of Mother Superior in the Sisters of No Mercy, her hand gently rubbing the side of her pregnant belly. "Like in that it is packed. Jammed."

"Jammed with what?"

Roxanne reaches for the epauletted black leather front-laced bustier hanging on the hook next to her jacket. "Ministerial stuff."

"Ministerial stuff? How could you possibly be jammed up with ministerial stuff? I was Minister of War and I was never jammed."

"Yeah, but that's only because you were doing it wrong," Roxanne says, stepping into the bustier and pulling it slowly up over her knees and then her hips.

Trip's left eyebrow goes up. "Wrong?"

"Okay, bad choice of words." Roxanne eases the bustier into place around her torso, favoring her bulging belly. She starts cinching the laces, keeping the ones around her stomach nice and loose. "You did it your way. You tended not to sweat the details. Or even the broad strokes."

"They call that efficiency."

"That's one way of putting it."

"That is the way I'm putting it."

"You know me. I'm just a little more conscientious about responsibilities."

"*Anal,* I think the word you're looking for is."

"Okay, sure, yes." Roxanne grabs her red patent leather stiletto boots, standing waiting against the wall, and plops down on the edge of the mattress. "But the thing is there are a lot of them. Responsibilities, I mean. Keeps my days pretty well packed."

"All right, so your days are spoken for. Cool, I get that. But it's not day right now."

"Well, you know how my days used to be pretty packed already with Mother Superior stuff..."

"And you haven't quit the Sisterhood."

"No. Couldn't if I wanted to. Sister for life." Roxanne slips the boots on, all the way up past her knees. "My Sisterhood stuff, those duties haven't gone away. Wouldn't want them to. They're important. Not just to me but to my sisters."

Trip nods. "I see where this is going."

"Yep. Since my days are spoken for by Minister of War duties, the Sisterhood stuff tends to speak for my nights. I've handed over what I can to Bernice, but there are some things only a Mother Superior can do."

"Which you have to do tonight? You can't skip a night?"

"New recruit orgy tonight. It isn't official if I'm not there to preside, and if it's not official, the new recruits won't qualify for their initiate vespers. And the vespers, those are the cornerstones to the entire experience."

"Can't do without those vespers, right."

"I'm sorry, Trip." She lays a hand on his thigh. "When I made the date with you I forgot about tonight. Can we do this tomorrow? I can free up tomorrow night."

"I don't know. The cheese might not keep. Truth be told, it probably is rad-rat milk cheese. You know Hunt-R, always with the shortcuts. And no qualms about lying to me. Wonder where he gets that from?"

"I'm okay if the cheese doesn't keep."

"It's not just the cheese," Trip says with a shrug. "I've got a schedule, too, you know. Jammed packed. And getting jammier."

"Really?"

"Really. Was gonna give Lock a visit, see what she's been up to."

"You've got a scheme brewing, don't you?"

"And it's a good one, too."

"You leaving in the morning?"

"I'd have to check my day planner, but yeah, I think that was the plan."

"You gonna come back, this time?" Roxanne asks. "Or are you going to put even more on my plate and make me hunt you down again?"

"I do like being hunted. Especially by you."

"*Trip*."

"I'll be back." He sets his hand on the curve of her belly. "Before this thing pops."

"You'd better be."

Trip hops off the mattress and grabs her cloak, hanging over the back of the chair in front of the work desk, piled high with salvaged electronics in varying degrees of disassembly. "Come on, I'll walk you to the temple," he says, offering her a hand to help her stand.

"You're going to try and get a peek at the orgy, aren't you?" Roxanne asks as she pulls herself to her feet.

Trip hands her the cloak with a devilish half-smile. "What do you think?"

CHAPTER ELEVEN

NOON and the harsh Wasteland sun is at its highest and harshest, not a cloud in the pale gray sky. The *Festering Wound* rips down the cracked and broken two-lane blacktop that runs parallel along the long-ago dried up Susquehanna, its pock-marked depleted uranium armor plates glinting in the sun.

"I mean, what even is the point?" Trip asks, interlocking his fingers behind his head and leaning back. Hand-rolled cig dangling on his bottom lip, the steering wheel makes WIFI mind-controlled micro-adjustments in synch with his rapidly twitching left eyebrow. "Why bother making a sequel if you're going to rip out everything that made the first one a classic to begin with?"

In the passenger seat, Rudy's got his T-shirt pulled up and is fiddling with his left nipple, a contented daze over his eyes. "A classic? Really?"

"Vishnu's receding hairline, are you shitting me?" Trip whips his head around. "You're honestly going to sit there and attempt to argue that *Tron* isn't one of the finest motion pictures ever made?"

"It was okay, dude." Rudy pinches his nipple, adding a squirt of LSD-analogue into his bloodstream. His dumb smile gets dumber as spectral colors start creeping in around the corner of his vision like sprinkle cupcake-tipped fingers reaching greedily for his rapidly dilating irises. "Just okay. Those graphics... so low-rez. And the acting—"

Trip interrupts. "Cindy Morgan never looked better than in that skin-tight neon jumpsuit."

Rudy shrugs and pulls his T-shirt down. "No argument here, but it was so cheesy, and what about that scene in the arcade where the three of them are talking and you can see the mic come up between them? A mic in shot. How did that even make it into a final cut on a frakking Disney film? One they spent actual money on?"

"The 80's were a weird time, I admit." Trip sucks his cig down to a lip-burning nub, then flicks it out the window. He immediately reaches into his tux jacket to pull another cig out of the tin, twitching his eyebrow to get the dashboard lighter warming up. "And okay, the film's got its problems, nobody's denying that, but you've got to look at it on a deeper level."

"Deeper level? It's a 16-bit *Wizard of Oz* riff. That's as deep as I need to dig."

"Sure, but this Oz is a place you actually want to spend time in." Trip lights the cig and tilts his head left, then right, his neck cracking. "The universe it depicts, that's what makes it a classic. Forget the acting, forget the plot holes, forget even the nonsensical blast-proof warehouse door–"

"Why does a software company need a blast-proof door?"

"Focus on that universe. A world inside a computer. And not just any world—the world the programs in the computer live and work and love and die in. Not a simulation of a world, mind you, but their actual world. The secret world of computer programs–accounting programs, game programs, you name it."

"Yeah, so?"

"*Yeah, so?* Do you not get how significant that is?"

"Obviously not." Rudy waves his fingers in front of his face. "But then again the hippy juice is kicking in. Either that or I've actually turned into liquid metal. I haven't, have I?"

"No, you're still the same old hairy lump of flesh and bone you've always been," Trip says. "And their world wasn't something someone programmed. It was internally, logically consistent, with laws and physics and social roles and norms that rose spontaneously up from the primordial calculator ooze and evolved on its own. An entire universe created not by the harsh realities of biological Darwinism but the harsh realities of digital Darwinism."

"With cool motorcycles."

"Lightcycles," Trip says, stabbing his cig at Rudy. "They're called lightcycles."

Rudy flinches at the cig, sure he is dodging a winged train barreling at him. "The sequel had lightcycles. And that Wilde chick in a skin-tight neon jumpsuit. Upgrade."

"But you know what it didn't have?"

"Mics in the shot?" Rudy says with a chuckle.

Trip ignores him. "It didn't have the same universe."

"Of course it did. The kid was Flynn's son. And it had computer programs running around inside a computer. That's the same universe."

"No, the *Tron* universe is actual programs running around inside a computer—a self-created proto-Internet slash cyberspace, a universe created by the interaction of millions of different programs, the underlying architecture of the CPU supporting it all, as well as providing its uniqueness. The *Tron Legacy* universe is simulated *people* running around inside a *simulation of the original's universe*. A simulation programmed by a human, with rules and laws coded to approximate the original, spontaneous universe, and divorced from any hardware it was running on."

"So what?"

"So, it was basically just a fancy Sim Life. I don't care how clever Flynn was, there was no way he could model into the simulated universe the inherent chaos system of the spontaneous universe. Making the simulated universe nothing more than a complex game. A mind wank. The programs didn't have any free will. Nothing they did mattered. It was all AI, created by a fallible man-child god."

"Ah, stakes." Rudy reaches out toward the dashboard. "Um... steaks. Come to papa," he says, grabbing up the hallucinatory plate of rare T-bone, baked potato, and ketchup, floating in the air in front of him.

"Yes, stakes," Trip says, twitching the *Wound* into a sharp right turn onto another two-laner. "When Tron killed the MCP in the first one, it mattered. He was saving a real universe. The programs had real sentience. Not artificial, not programmed by any god except those they invented themselves, limited only by hardware constraints."

"I see you've given this a lot of thought," Rudy says, furiously cutting into his imaginary steak with an imaginary knife and forking big chunks of imaginary ketchup-drenched imaginary meat into his mouth. "Too much, one might say. I say that."

"It has kept me up at nights," Trip says with a thoughtful sigh. "Well, okay not that but the whole probing the dark memory zone inside my implant, but after a while my mind drifts inevitably to thoughts of how much I hate *Tron Legacy*, if only for the wasted potential. And for not having any actual Tron in it."

Rudy's imaginary fork, loaded with imaginary potato, pauses at his lips and he looks over at his brother. "Wait a sec, there. It did have Tron. That Rinzler guy. He turned out to be Tron. Somehow."

"No, it had some last-minute post-production tinkering and an ADR line about fighting for the users thrown in, as an afterthought." Trip plucks an onion ring from Rudy's plate and pops it into his mouth. "It's a frakking *Tron* movie – don't you think it should have gone without saying that it should have some actual Tron in it, for Shatner's sake? And don't even get me started on the music."

Rudy watches his brother chew, very confused. "Yeah, that I did find weird. The music from the first one, that's like iconic."

"And what did *Legacy* give us?" Trip asks, wiping his mouth with the back of his seven-fingered claw. "New music. Bah. And only a few tinny notes of the original score from a toy. What, they couldn't have done a remix of the original theme over the end credits? Even *Star Trek* got at least that right."

"*Oy, vey,* that *Star Trek* reboot."

"Yeah, Kelvin timeline can suck it." Trip's voice trails off as he looks out the windshield and down the road, a rising dust cloud on the horizon. "Um... You did say Lock set up shop in Billtown, right?"

"Yeah, that's what Bernie told me," Rudy says, putting his plate and utensils in the dishwasher that's appeared inside the glove compartment.

Trip scowls at the shapes inside the dust cloud. Tall, shining spires of nano-machine manipulated steel surrounded by a two-story high wall of concrete. "I didn't know Billtown had a city."

"You were expecting ramshackle, weren't you?"

"It's the Wasteland, of course I was expecting ramshackle."

"It was a ramshackle. Then Lock and her ex-zombie army moved in." Rudy squints out the front window at the approaching city. And the laughing demon giants lined up behind it, waiting for him. He reaches under his shirt and pinches his nipple twice, backing off on the LSD flow. "And made... that. I am seeing that, right?"

"Yeah, you're seeing that. Well, minus the demons. No demons."

"Cool... wait. Did I mention the demons? I don't remember mentioning the demons."

"Don't worry about it," Trip says. He whistles in appreciation at his pseudo-daughter's city. "So in six months, they built that?"

"Lock built the All-Mart – she knows a few things about building rapidly. And, apparently, massively."

"Well, I wanted to get some industrious zombie-like workers."

"Looks like we came to the right place," Rudy nods, then sinks down into his seat, chewing his thumbnail nervously. "Except for the demons. I do not like the look of them. They could be Belgian —we will have to be on our guard."

CHAPTER TWELVE

"SIR, IT'S TIME," Brenda says as she opens the heavy blinds and lets the sunlight stream into the private chamber at the top of the highest tower in Lock's city-state.

The shaft of light strikes the pool of gray goo in the center of the chamber. The goo ripples, tendrils of the thick liquid spearing out towards a central point, a mouth with delicate lips forming on the surface of the sphere the tendrils form.

"You know you don't have to call me 'sir'?" Lock's lips say, the rest of her body rising from the pool, formed by hundreds of finger-thick tendrils of nanochines shooting up from the pool, writhing together to make a torso, arms, belly.

Brenda walks to the edge of the pool. Around the periphery of the chamber stand Lock's attendants, a cross-section of the Combine's population selected at random for the honor, their backs respectfully turned to their queen. "It's good that the others hear it, if only to remind them of the hierarchy."

Her hips and thighs emerging from the pool, fine, wispy tendrils snake out from her scalp to sculpt out Lock's eyes, hers ears and nose forcing themselves into being. "I doubt they'll forget the hierarchy. Most of them have been with me for years."

"And most of that time as mind-controlled slaves," Brenda says. "They're no longer under your mental influence."

"Oh, they're still under my influence," Lock says with a sly smile, her body lifting almost fully out of the pool, her feet and toes forming, her skin developing life-like pores and a smattering of calculated imperfections.

"You know what I meant. They no longer have your nanochines coursing through their blood."

"Are you saying I should start questioning their loyalty?" Lock steps out of the pool, her arms outstretched. Tendrils in the pool form a robe, thick and brocaded, other tendrils lifting the robe out and draping it over her. "Because if we're at that point, I could just slip some nanochines into the food supply and put an end to any nascent revolution right now."

"I don't think that will be necessary, sir." Brenda helps Lock button the front of the robe, then cinches the wide belt. "I've seen no signs that the people's adoration and dedication to you is faltering. In fact, it is probably stronger now than when you were their All-Mart."

"Then why the whole 'sir' business, Marcie?"

Brenda's head jogs slightly, indicating the attendants surrounding them. "It's not yours and their place in the hierarchy I would like to remind them of."

"Ah, got it." Lock's skin ripples, transitioning from gray to take on a deep golden bronze sheen. White spreads out over her gray eyes, a burst of the reddest-red flashing out to color her irises. "Well, go pick a few at random and have them killed as an example. Trust me, that'll leave them no doubt who my second-in-command is."

"Sir, we talked about this," Brenda says. "Random killing of your own subjects is on the no-no list."

"A list I don't remember agreeing to abide by."

"You did. Or I leave. That was the deal."

"Like you'd ever go trade in the big combine lights and action and go back to that shithole of a sinkhole Shunk."

"The Cthulists are always recruiting."

"You won't let me give you your own nanochines so you can transform that vulnerable meat-bod of yours into something more practical, but you'd let those genetically engineered multi-dimensional-demon worshiping freaks turn you into a veggie-pus? Maybe I should let you go, if your judgment is that bad."

Brenda sighs. "Are we ready to go over today's schedule, or would you like to banter some more?"

"Pencil some more banter in for after lunch." Lock raises her hand, fanning out her fingers just the slightest. Behind her, thick tendrils rise from the pool, slushing together to rapidly form a wide, high-backed chair. Without looking, Lock takes two steps back and sits, just as the throne completes weaving itself. "We're still on for lunch, right?"

"Of course," Brenda says, reaching into the weathered leather bag at her hip. She pulls out a small notebook, kept shut by a dozen rubber bands. "But before that, there's a rather busy schedule ahead of you."

"Don't know if I like the sound of that," Lock says, feigning a yawn. "Tell you what. Clear the decks. Nothing until after our after-lunch banter. We'll go driving, or something. Get some fresh-ish Wasteland air, maybe find some non-subjects who aren't covered by the no-no list and mind-control them into fighting each other to the death."

Brenda rolls the rubber bands off the notebook, stuffing them away in the pocket of her jacket, the sharp striped one with the epaulets and flared collar. She flips the notebook open. "As tempting as that sounds, we can't clear the decks entirely."

"If you say I have to inspect the tank factory again, I swear I'm going to nanochine you and make you dance the dance of a thousand veils for my puerile enjoyment."

"Like you need to nanochine me to do that," Brenda says with a playful bob of her head. "But no, no tank inspection today. Even though the retrofit of the tank factory's a lynchpin to our plans, and you stopping by to check on the progress would be a huge morale builder to the workers and management alike."

"I'll send them a nice signed painting of me they can hang on the factory entrance archway, you know, so I can greet them in spirit every morning when they show up for work."

"They've already got one. Maybe they can hang the new one in the bathroom."

"Wow, you are really begging for nanochines today, aren't you?"

"Or maybe I'm just advocating spruced-up bathrooms. There isn't a room your picture couldn't brighten."

"Can't argue with that. Okay, so no tank factory inspection. We can go driving."

"The new prototype is ready."

"Ooh, it's test day?"

"It's test day."

"Why didn't you say so before?" Lock asks, leaning forward. "You know how I love me my test day."

"Yes, sir."

"Okay, let's go test." Lock slides off the throne and marches for the door, an attendant opening it for her. Half-way there, she stops and turns around to look at Brenda, standing there facing the throne, reading her notebook. "And you're not following me. Why are you not following me? Is not my child-like enthusiasm so infectious it just makes you want to both scurry along after me unquestioningly and puke your ever-loving guts out?"

"There is one other matter."

"And you suspect it's not going to fill me with feelings of utter joy?" Lock spins around on her heel. "Is it about bunnies? I bet it's about bunnies. Stupid bunnies. They get into the power-plant wiring again, gain radioactive superpowers, and go on a killing spree? Wait, that might actually be worth seeing."

Brenda looks over her shoulder at Lock. "Your father and uncle showed up at the front gate an hour ago."

"And you're only telling me this now because...?"

"It's been six months, and you didn't exactly part with them on the best of terms."

"What, just because I was going to kill that woman of his?"

"Yes. Because you were going to kill the Mother Superior. His woman."

"Would have been a mercy killing. Anyway, I didn't. Did he say what he wants?"

Brenda lowers her voice and grumbles out, "Revenge."

"Really? He said that?"

"Nah, just kidding. He's got a business proposal."

"Of course he does."

Brenda nods. "Probably some donkey-brained idea that'll go nowhere and end in lost investment for you, embarrassment for him, and tragedy for the planet in general."

"Still, I should probably see him," Lock says.

"I can bump them to tomorrow, get them a nice room in the cheaper motel."

"No, I'll see them this morning."

"What about the test?"

"They can come," Lock says. "There's always room in my schedule to rub things in."

CHAPTER THIRTEEN

"YOU WANT WHAT?" Lock asks, leaning back to let the swarm of attendants remove plates and utensils, clearing the table for after-lunch coffee and fruit. Except for Rudy's plate—he bats away all efforts to take his plate, grunting while he gnaws at a chicken leg with one hand, grabbing the rest of the chicken with the other before it's taken away.

"A thousand zombie workers," Trip says, slugging down his coffee as soon as the attendant's finished filling it. He holds it out for another top off. "And hard workers. Don't try to unload all your slackers on me. That's not going to be a problem, is it?"

"Not for me," Lock says. Standing behind her, Brenda cups her hand to her ear and mumbles something into her throat mike.

"Good... good," Trip says. He downs half the coffee this time, but instead of waving for a refill, he plucks the pot from the attendant's hand. The attendant stares at him for a moment, then shrugs, backing away. Trip starts spooning sugar into his cup, spoon after heaping spoon. "About time my luck changed."

Lock gives him a bemused look across the table. "Oh, it didn't change. It's not a problem for me. Just for you. Even if they would voluntarily leave my service, which they won't, because I'm me, and they love me more than their own lives, I can't spare the workers."

"Okay, then ten," Trip says, giving the coffee a quick stir, making a sludge. He fills the cup up the rest of the way, to the very brim, and holds it up to his lips, pinky out. "I'll settle for ten."

"I don't think you're getting it," Lock says. She turns to Rudy, pulling at a chicken carcass for any meat he can get. "I don't think he's getting it."

Rudy shakes his head and says around a mouthful of chicken, "He's not getting it."

"I'm not getting it," Trip admits. "What could you possibly need all these zombies for? You've built your city, it's nice, but how much bigger does it need to be? And I don't know if you've noticed, but while you've been building this place there's a war going on out there. It's downright selfish to be hogging all this zombie labor on what amounts to a vanity project when they could be contributing to the war effort."

"By building your little war cars?" Lock asks.

"Megacars. I'm calling them megacars."

"So let me see I've got this straight. You want me to give you zombies so they can build war cars for you. Which you will then sell?"

"Capitalism's sorta my bag."

"Purely for self-defense, I take it?"

"I just make 'em and sell them at a ridiculous war-economy profiteering margin. What they get used for is entirely up to the buyer. I make no moral judgments." Trip slurps down the last of the sludge. "I'm above all that rigamarole."

Lock smirks. "Except when you're trying to guilt me into giving you some free labor."

"Whatever works." Trip looks up from dumping sugar into his empty cup, arching an eyebrow. "Did it work?"

"No, of course it didn't work," Lock says. "It just makes me double-down on the whole 'nope' thing. Why would I give free labor to a competitor?"

"A what?"

"A competitor," Lock says, fanning her fingers at the coffee pot next to Trip's elbow. The table sprouts a tendril, picking up the tea-pot, and tipping it over Trip's cup to fill it. "Not a serious competitor, but still, who needs a roadside banana stand hawking rotten fruit in the parking lot of the nice shiny big box store? Don't need you annoying my customers."

"Rotten fruit? I'll have you know these megacars are going to be state-of-the-art, for 1943, and perfectly suited for the kind of rough-and-tumble bang-bang boom-boom slap-your-fanny-and-sing-Matilda war faring challenges of the modern post-apocalyptic battlefield. —Rudy, show her the blueprints."

"Um, no blueprints, but I do have some napkin sketches."

"Then show her the napkin sketches."

Lock shakes his head. "I don't need to see the sketches."

"She says she doesn't need to see the sketches," Rudy says, eyeing up a tray of sliced oranges an attendant holds out to him.

Trip shrugs. "Back up a sec. What was that you said about customers?" he asks, a rumble sounding from somewhere outside the room. "What the hell are you selling?"

Lock smiles and nods at the far wall. It parts down the middle, the stones becoming like liquid, folding back into themselves until all that is left is an open archway to the street—a street filled with marching machines.

"Those," Lock says, pointing out at the machines: Twenty feet tall, armor plated walking tanks, some with shoulder-mounted missile clusters, others with chainsaws for hands, each piloted by a man or woman safely encased in an armored chest cavity.

Rudy turns around in his seat, an orange slice inches from his lips. "Are those?"

"Yes," Lock says.

Rudy pops the slice into his mouth. "Oh, those are sweet."

"Mecha?" Trip coughs out, spitting coffee over his traveling tuxedo's lapels. "You've been building mecha?"

"Building and selling," Brenda says. "Like hotcakes. Everybody wants them. The Chinese. The Free Mexicans. The Pocono Regulars. Even got an order from Shunk for two last week."

"From Shunk?" Trip asks. "Really?"

"So now do you see why I can't spare the labor?" Lock says. "I'm going to have to add a second shift to keep up with demand—maybe a third once we move into production with mark two."

"You've already got a mark two?" Rudy asks.

"We're testing it today," Lock says. "It's going to blow the market wide open. Nobody else has anything like it."

"What, does it fly?" Trip asks with a disparaging chuckle.

"Yes," Lock says.

"Like, *fly* fly?" Rudy asks.

"Should be able to do better than supersonic," Brenda says.

Rudy lets out a soft whistle. "Shit."

"Bullshit," Trip says. He starts dumping spoonful after spoonful of sugar into his already full cup, the sugar not sinking, instead just piling up on top of the already sludgy brew. "Flying doesn't work. Nobody flies. Anything faster than a dirigible gets higher than a hundred feet and *blam*, Death From Above."

"I know, I know, that's been a problem," Lock says. "But I think I licked it."

"How?" asks Rudy, wide-eyed.

"Aww, unc, trade secret," Lock says. "Let's just say I'm a frickin' genius."

Trip glares at her. "Bull. Shit."

Brenda cups her hand over her ear again. "Sir, they're ready for the word," she announces.

"The word is given," Lock says, fanning her fingers at the ceiling. The stones ripple soundlessly, peeling back to reveal the open sky, cloudless and blue. "Second test flight. Fingers crossed."

"What happened to the first test flight?" Rudy asks, looking up.

Lock puts a finger against her lips and looks skyward.

With a high-pitched rumbling roar, a mecha with delta wings where its arms should be shoots by overhead, cones of blue fire erupting from its thigh-mounted thrusters. The mecha-jet climbs quickly, higher and higher, a straight line—

And then *blam*. Death From Above.

The beam looks like a shaft of solid blued steel, slicing down through the sky with the crackle of ozone set ablaze.

The beam's there for two, maybe three, tenths of a second. Long enough to turn the mecha-jet into a puff of particles, none bigger than the tip of a thumb.

The particles rain down on the towers and streets of Lock's Combine.

"That," Lock says. "That's pretty much what happened to the first test flight." She raises a fist to the sky, extending her middle finger. "Fuck you. Just fuck you."

"Told you it was bullshit," Trip says, spooning coffee sugar sludge into his mouth.

"Lasted longer than the first test, sir," Brenda says, placing a hand on Lock's shoulder. "We'll get there."

Lock puts her own hand over Brenda's. "We'd better. We've already got over a thousand pre-orders."

"A thousand?" Trip blurts, sending sludge spitting out over the table.

Lock sags back into her chair, the ceiling weaving itself shut above them. "I know, I was expecting more by this point, but I guess some people want to see some actual flying first before plunking down the half-mil deposit. Even with my track record of unparalleled success."

"You're getting how much?" Trip asks.

"It's one of those if you have to ask you can't afford it things," Lock says.

"The recovery team reports they've found the wreckage," Brenda announces.

"Bring it in for analysis and tell the engineering team to expect me this afternoon. There's a lot of work to do." Lock smiles at Trip. "So, Trip, care to lend a hand? We could use your expertise?"

"I'm not gonna be your sales manager, Lock." Trip puts down his cup and wipes his mouth with a cloth napkin. As soon as he puts it down an attendant takes the used napkin away, replacing it with a clean one. "V.P. of sales, maybe, if you throw in the COO and CEO spots."

"I was thinking more code tester," Lock says. "You're good with that low-level stuff. —And he's storming off."

On his way to the door, Trip yells back over his shoulder. "By the way, I hate the new skin color! Makes you look like an over-roasted turkey."

Lock watches until the attendants close the door behind Trip, then turns to Rudy. "So, unc, how's the wife and kids?"

CHAPTER FOURTEEN

THE *WOUND* ROARS away from the Combine, towards the setting sun, the Dodge's adaptive tires kicking up twin trails of dust behind her.

"You believe the nerve of that egotistical, self-centered, nano-chine-infested freak?" Trip asks, his hands clawed around the car's steering wheel, his knuckles white, the wireless jack behind his ear blinking an agitated red—no link. He's doing this manual, and the *Wound*'s puppy-level AI is not happy about it, wondering what it did wrong. "I've got half a mind to invent a practical method for time travel, build a time machine using those principles, put on a snazzy jumpsuit, hurdle back through time to our happy-go-lucky early teens, and stop ourselves from accidentally setting off that All-Mart bomb and creating her in the first place."

In the passenger seat, Rudy's got his stomach unzipped, his hand rummaging inside his guts. "If we had a time machine, I'd go back to stop George Lucas from casting Hayden Christensen."

Trip glances sideways at his brother. "What, you wouldn't stop him from doing the whole Jar-Jar thing?"

"I like Jar-Jar," Rudy says, popping the empty vial of raw hallucinogenic ingredients out of his belly-implanted chem synth plant with a hiss. He flicks the empty vial out the open window. "He's funny."

"Remind me to get a DNA test at some point. No way we can actually be brothers." Trip turns his attention back to the road, ignoring the flashing GameGear screen in the dashboard, pleading to establish a link. "But the correct plan is to stop the prequels entirely... and then stop ourselves from setting off the All-Mart bomb."

Rudy takes a pair of glasses — older than he is by a factor of three, kept together with electrical tape and wire, the left lens cracked, the other one discolored with age — out of what used to be a hideaway knife sheath in his right combat boot, and slips them on.

"Okay," he says, adjusting his bandolier so he can squint down his nose through the glasses to read the labels on the lids of the vials of chem mixes stored in it. "So we didn't get the workers we need. We can build some robots to do the work. You'll see. It'll work out."

"Nobody's building any robots." The flashing plea for a connection on the screen gets flashier, with reds and yellows, and now a soft but insistent beep. Trip rolls his eyes and reaches for the screen and it's big flashing CONNECT button. At the last second, he pokes the physical OFF button instead and the screen goes black. "Nobody's building anything. What's the point?"

"Sure, Lock's mechas are sweet, but they're high-end. Not everybody's going to be able to afford them." Rudy scans the vial labels, with names like SKYWALKER KUSH - BEGGAR'S CANYON REMIX (THC-A/MESC-A), LORD OF THE HIGHS (THC-A/PEYOTE DISTILLATE), and DON'T EVER USE THIS ONE, IT WILL KILL YOU (SERIOUSLY). "We can serve the low-end market. Warcars for the warlord on a budget."

"Warcars? You saw what I saw. She's got a jet," Trip says through clenched teeth. "A flying jet."

"Yeah, so?" Rudy selects a vial labeled SURPRISE ME and pushes it out of the bandolier with his thumb. "It couldn't make it to a thousand feet before it got blown away. Nobody's going to buy a jet that can't fly, it's useless."

"Today it couldn't make it to a thousand feet. Today it's useless. But she'll figure it out. And she'll do it sooner than later. It's inevitable."

Rudy jams the vial in through the zippered opening in his belly and attaches it to the synth implant with a twist of his wrist. A hiss and a gentle whine of pumps coming online tell him it's in place. "She is a frickin' genius."

"Chip off the old block," Trip says, knocking a knuckle against his temple, a slight begrudgingly proud smile on his long face. "And once she does figure it out, and her jets can fly, really fly, that's it, end of line."

"You really think jets will change the war-machine business all that much?" Rudy zips up his stomach, then sits back, wiping the viscera on his hand off on his jeans. "They'll still be awfully expensive. There'll be a low-end niche for us."

Trip glares out at the road, and the setting sun. "For maybe a year, two, max. Then the sea-change will really hit. Jet flight is too important, too much of a game-changer. Everybody will want in. Every government already out there, and every wannabe government, they're going to need an air force. To defend against everybody else's air force, and to do what governments invariably do, try to take over other governments. Jets turn every other type of warfare into a joke. What good is sending a tank—or a warcar—into battle when a jet can get there, drop a couple dozen bombs, and be back before the tank's left the parking lot?"

"Okay, maybe we make boats then. Always wanted to build a destroyer." Rudy taps his left nipple twice to prime the new vial pumping, then puts his elbow out the window while he waits for whatever effect it turns out to be to kick in. "And the kids would love living on a coast."

"You're missing the bigger picture. Once flight's back in the picture, every government is going to want—and absolutely need—an air force, and then boom you've got yourself an instant new market. At first, Lock'll have that market sewn up. But the market will be too big, even for her and her zombies. Big markets create competition. Big markets create pressure to innovate. Pressure to reduce prices. And the promise of profits. Huge profits. Every corp, big and small, is going to suddenly be in the jet business, and they'll have to pivot, because nobody will want the old shit. The tanks and the warcars and the mechs, they'll be gathering dust overnight. And while they're gathering dust, all the resources of all those corps are going to be focused on one thing: figuring out how Lock did it. Why her planes don't get shot out of the sky."

Rudy drums his fingers on the side of the door impatiently, his head starting to feel uncomfortably clear. "Somebody's going to reverse engineer."

"Of course. All those resources, it's gonna happen. So fast it'll leave Lock whiplashed." Trip pushes in the dashboard lighter and takes out a cig. "And then it's floodgates open."

"Everybody will be making jets."

"Not just jets." The dashboard lighter pops and Trip lights his cig. "Missiles. Rockets. Anything that usually gets blown out of the sky will be fair game again. And then it's game over."

"There are other businesses we can be in," Rudy says, squirming in his seat. He's sweating now. He puts his hand over his stomach—the synth factory is on, humming away. Just ain't doing anything for him yet. And now he's getting a headache, too. "Robot nannies, for instance."

"I'm not talking game over for our business," Trip says. "I'm talking game over for civilization. Again. And this time, it may be final."

Rudy pokes at his belly, frowning. "I don't follow."

"Allow me to lead you there, then. Planet's basically been in a constant state of war since the First Reboot, right?"

Sweat drips down Rudy's face, and his head pounds. "Right, 'cause humans are petty, selfish, and generally enjoy being unpleasant to each other."

"Yep. But the wars have been, compared to the Big One that led to the First Reboot, relatively minor affairs—Little Ones. Low-speed things. Tanks and swords and trebuchets and walking tree soldiers. The kind of thing that leads to small, regional reboots. No mass *mass* destruction. At the end of the war, maybe a country or two's left in ruin, and certainly there are casualties, but overall, the rest of the world chugs on its own merry way, until another of the always-brewing regional conflicts boils over. At which point the cycle repeats itself. It's not the best situation, but it's kept humanity mostly alive and kicking, if not progressing, for the better part of two centuries. It's not peace, but it is in its own way stability. And you know why it's been like that? Why wars don't threaten to end all life as we know it anymore?"

Sweat drips into Rudy's mouth, tasting of bitter salt, and the pounding headache gains a ringing tinnitus accompaniment. "Um... people are slowly becoming less petty, selfish, and amused by being unpleasant to each other?"

"Not by a longshot," Trip says. "People are people. They're always going to be assholes. That'll never change. Nor should it. It's what defines us as a species."

Rudy looks down at his bandolier, notices a few of the edges of the vial labels are curled and loose. "Speaking of assholes, did you change my labels?"

"While you were asleep," Trip says with a smiling nod. "Mixed 'em up good."

Rudy glares at him. "You don't happen to remember which one you changed SURPRISE ME to, do you? It's supposed to be a nice gently bubbly high. This is not bubbly at all. I'm having hot flashes. My tongue is freezing. It's like Philip Glass is warming up in my ears while the Blue Man Group is playing on my brain stage. And I can feel my knees. Why can I feel my knees, Trip?"

"Uh, I think I swapped that one with the IT WILL KILL YOU one."

"Seriously? You dick," Rudy says, then shoves his head out the window to let the air whisk away some of the sweat drenching him.

"What?" Trip asks, keeping his eyes on the road. "The implant has safeties. No mix is really gonna kill you."

"No, but it's doing a pretty good job detoxing me." Rudy pulls his head back in and quickly closes the window, suddenly feeling cold. He wraps his arms around his chest and shivers. "Which is frankly worse than killing me."

Trip shrugs. "Just switch vials then."

"Can't. It's a flush-cycle clean-out detox mix."

"Why the fuck would you make one of those in the first place?"

"Bernie made me whip it up, for the next time we can swing a date night. I interrupt it before it's done, I'm down and out with what amounts to the bends for a month, and I blow the gaskets on the synth's pumps. And you know how hard it is to get replacement gaskets for this thing? I don't feel like schlepping it to Zimbabwe again."

"How long's the cycle?"

"Four to eight days," Rudy says his teeth chattering. "Depending on how hard I've been running the motor, lately."

"So eight days of no drugs, then?"

"Yeah. Did I mention you're a dick?"

"Want a cig?"

"Can't." Rudy reaches for the heater, sliding it to max. "The nic will interact with the detox agents and give me herpes."

Trip switches the heater off. "You don't have herpes already?"

"Go ahead. Laugh it up, monkey-boy. But just remember, the only reason I normally don't just outright strangle you is because I'm stoned enough to deal with your bullshit."

Trip's smile turns into a satisfied smirk and he stabs a finger at the GameGear, switching it back on. Another stab, this time at the button on the flashing screen, and he lets the *Wound*'s puppy-AI connect to his mind. There's a palpable sense of relief from over the connection, and Trip lets go of the wheel, lacing his fingers behind his neck and leaning back as the *Wound* takes over, accelerating gleefully into the next curve. "Now where was I? Oh, yeah, I'll tell you why wars don't threaten to end all life as we know it anymore: Death From Above."

"Death From Above?"

"Death From Above," Trip repeats, his voice a reverent whisper. "Who knows what it is, or why it does what it does, but thank Shatner it does do what it does, which is keep the skies free of jets. And missiles. And intercontinental rockets. Especially intercontinental rockets. Take Death From Above out of the picture and before long, you've got a planet that's literally flying willy-nilly at supersonic speeds to the next Big One. And the next Big One, there's a good chance we won't get a reboot after it. Civilization ain't what it used to be. Totally not as resilient. It could just be the end. Power down and off."

"Well, that's not good," Rudy says, his face pale, his hair soaked with his own sweat.

"*Eh*, it is what it is. Humans had a pretty good run."

"Wait, with all this talk, I thought you were building up steam for something. Like convincing Lock to stop trying to figure out jets."

"No, I was just making small talk."

"We've got to do something," Rudy says, back to being uncomfortably hot. He rolls down his window. "Think about the kids. Their future."

Trip glances over at him, arching an eyebrow. "Kids? What kids?"

"All the kids. My kids. *Your* incoming kid."

"Oh, yeah. Keep forgetting about them. Well, I guess... if we must, we could try and stop the war."

"Stop the war?" Rudy takes the glasses off, shoving them back in their boot sheath, and rubs his temples with his palms. "Stop the war... right. Yeah... I get it. We stop the war, Lock's market goes away, and she stops working on jets. Or at least slows down. Buys us some time to try to convince her to abandon her research."

"What? Like Lock would ever listen to me? Anyway, stopping the war won't stop the future, and jets are the future. If it isn't Lock, it'll be somebody who figures it out. No, we stop the war because it's the right thing to do."

"Because you started the war in the first place?"

"I would say that's open to historical interpretation," Trip says, dashing his cig out in the ashtray. "But no, I was more thinking that it's only right that if anybody's going to profit from the war, it should be me. Definitely not Lock. Screw her and her patronizing code tester offer."

"So you want to stop the war to spite Lock?"

"And cut off her profit line."

"Of course."

"Cut her off, and at the same time, make a little profit for ourselves."

I'm almost afraid to ask... how are we going to make a profit off of stopping the war?"

"A little thing called diplomacy, brother." Trip's left eyebrow twitches and the dashboard lighter pops in. "Something I'm so good at, and something so desperately needed in these troubled times, that I am certain I can ask any price, and there will be suckers aplenty to gladly pay it."

"You are truly a monster."

Trip grabs the lighter when it pops and lights a fresh cig. "Also open to historical interpretation," he says, twitching again to hit the gas.

CHAPTER FIFTEEN

"ALL RIGHT, just park your vehicle and join the line there," the tall, green-skinned Cthulist guard says, bending down to address Trip through the *Wound*'s open window as the car slows to a stop in front of the enclave's main gate. The Cthulist guard points the tip of his spear-scythe at the dozens of refugees lined up at a door, just to the side of the gate, set into the hulking wall of interwoven ivy and tree branches surrounding the sacred village. "Once you're inside, change in to the provided robe and you'll be a Cthulist before you know it."

"Yeah, yeah, that's great, but we don't want to convert," Trip says, twitching to put the *Wound* into idle. "We're here to see your major-domo."

The guard's face tentacles quiver, taken aback. "You wish an audience with the reverent Mugatham'mmmrrrrr?"

"Yep." Trip slides a nic-caff-and-lizard-urine pill out of his Bugs Bunny PEZ and onto his tongue. "A pow-wow, yeah."

"The reverent Mugatham'mmmrrrrr does not have audiences with just anyone," the guard says. He looks back at the line of cars, trucks, and horse-drawn wagons clogging the road behind the *Wound*. "Many supplicants come to him, but most are turned away, for he is busy waging the Holy War. Unless he is expecting you. Is he expecting you?"

"I'm no supplicant. And I'm always expected. By everyone." Trip slips the PEZ away into his inner tux chest pocket. "Name's Trip."

The guard grunts, then yells over his shoulder into the shack behind him. "Jivllrrrle'remmm, is there a 'Trip' on the list?"

"There is no 'Trip' on the list, Dure'relementrrrrmmm," comes the answer out of the open shack window.

Dure'relementrrrrmmm shows a mouthful of pointed teeth to Trip. "You are not on the list."

"What do you mean I'm not on the list?" Trip asks. "This is some exclusionary bullshit, I'll tell you what. It's because I don't have tentacles, isn't it?"

"If you became one of us, you would need no permission to enter the sacred village," Dure'relementrrrrmmm says. "It would be your rightful home, as all of the sacred villages would be, and you could come and go as you please. There are other benefits to conversion, as well, not the least of which is assuring yourself a place on one of the Five Comets of Nirvana that will arrive after we cleanse the world of the human-folk and usher in the Old Age Reborn with our mass sacrificial suicide. Can I sign you up for conversion? There are still a few slots open before lunch."

"Thanks but no. I'm good." Trip thumbs over at Rudy, huddled knee-to-chest in the passenger seat, a glistening sheen of sweat on his forehead, a thousand-yard stare to his eyes. "You can check the list for Rudy, though."

"That is Rudy?" Dure'relementrrrrmmm asks, peering into the car. "He does not look well."

"That coming from a guy with tentacles growing out of his ears and fish-breath," Trip says, waving the air in front of his nose. "Just hold the judgment and check the list, will you?"

Dure'relementrrrrmmm grunts and calls into the shack again. "Jivllrrrle'remmm, is there a 'Rudy' on the list?"

"There is no 'Rudy' on the list, Dure'relementrrrrmmm."

"He is not on the list, either," Dure'relementrrrrmmm says to Trip. "Now, please, if you're not interested in conversion, pull over, turn around, and drive away. You are holding up the line and the convert applicants. We have a quota to meet."

"Hold on, hold on," Trip says, raising a hand in protest. "Me and Mugatham'mmmrrrrr's kid Brad go way back. Just get on the horn or the vine or whatever it is you guys use to talk to each other and mention my name to Brad. You'll see."

"It is a genetically-engineered internal organ, modified from what was once our spleen, to act as a conduit for short-wave radio transmissions over which we send coded signals, generated by another genetically-engineered internal organ, what was once our appendix."

"What are you talking about?" Trip asks.

"What we use to communicate over long distances. You seemed curious. I was just elaborating."

"I may have seemed curious, but trust me, that was purely tangential." Trip points at the Cthulist's stomach. "So can you get on this spleen network of yours and call Brad?"

"I could... but I will not." Dure'relementrrrrmmm says. "High Holy General Bradulithuni'mmmrrrrr is much too busy in the field leading the Holy Army of Ultimate Conversion against the treacherous and ungodly forces of the Chinese Occupation to be bothered by the likes of me."

"All right, how about spleening up Mugatham'mmmrrrrr himself? If he knew we are out here, he'd invite us in." Trip turns to smile at Rudy. "I'm sure he's forgotten that whole me hitting on his wife thing, right?"

Rudy lets out a low moan.

"I will not bother the reverent Mugatham'mmmrrrrr about this. You are not on the list. There is nothing I can do." Dure'relementrrrrmmm says, laying a hand over his spleen. "Now turn around and drive away, human, or do I need to have you and your car *thrown* away?"

A rustle off to the left gets Trip's attention. A section of the wall of leaves and branches shakes, parting like a curtain to let a massive tree, with roots writhing like tentacles, glide out towards the Dodge. It slows to a stop, looming over the hood.

"Hold up, hold up," Trip says, nodding a hello at the tree. "Tell you what. You let us in, I'll give you what we got in back."

"What is in the back?" Dure'relementrrrrmmm asks.

Trip's eyebrow twitches and the *Wound*'s trunk pops open with a sharp click. "Beer. The Wasteland's finest. Straight from Shunk. Twenty gallons of it."

Rudy suddenly becomes animated, lifting his head to glare at Trip. "We had beer in the car this whole time and you didn't tell me?"

Trip smirks at him. "What, I didn't mention it?"

"You bastard," Rudy says, and sinks back down into his knee-hugging, rocking-back-and-forth, sweat-drenched moaning.

"What do you say?" Trip asks Dure'relementrrrrmmm, turning away from Rudy with a cold shrug. "You and your fellow grunts tie one on tonight courtesy of yours truly, and in return you open the gate for us. Everybody's happy."

"We are Cthulists," Dure'relementrrrrmmm says. "We do not pollute our bodies with swill."

"Had to ask," Trip says, lighting a cig. "Tell you what, take it anyway. Use it for fuel, dump it out, I don't care. Just dead weight, really."

Rudy lets out a deep, sad moan.

Dure'relementrrrrmmm squints into the car at Rudy. "Are you sure he's all right?"

"Yeah, he's just being a big baby, can't deal with a little—" Trip cuts himself off sharply, seeing the concern in Dure'relementr-rrrmmm's deep-set eyes. "Oh, no, he's like dying. Could pass on to the next life any minute. Probably nothing can save him except advanced bio-medical hoodoo, and you know how rare that is." Trip pats Rudy on the shoulder. "Sorry, buddy."

"But we do advanced bio-medical hoodoo here!" Dure'rele-mentrrrrmmm announces.

"Really?" Trip asks with a sardonic grin. "Wow, that's a lucky coincidence. You hear that, Rudy? You're going to live! Live, I say! Oh, but wait. We're not on the list. That is just tragic. So close. And with all those kids at home depending on you. Well, too bad. You want thrown unceremoniously in the first ditch we come across, or you want to go the full cremated on a funeral pyre and then we toss your ashes into the first ditch we come across?"

"How about neither?" Rudy asks.

"I'm not driving around with your piss-smelling corpse rotting away in the passenger seat."

"Why is my corpse gonna smell like piss?"

"I'm gonna piss on it, obviously."

"Wait," Dure'relementrrrrmmm says. "This tragedy may be avoidable."

"Do tell," Trip says, tapping ashes out the window. And over Dure'relementrrrrmmm's woven boots.

Dure'relementrrrrmmm sneers at the cig as he calls back over his shoulder into the guard shack. "Jivllrrrle'remmm, is there not an exception to the entry rules for medical emergencies?"

"There is an exception for medical emergencies, Dure'rele-mentrrrrmmm."

"You see," Dure'relementrrrrmmm says. "We can let you in."

"That's fantastic," Trip says flatly.

"To seek medical assistance at the Hoodoo center, only," Dure'relementrrrrmmm says.

"Of course, of course." Trip holds his hand out to the Cthulists, his pinky extended. "We'll drive straight there. Pinky promise."

Dure'relementrrrrmmm hooks his boneless pinky with Trip's. "Take care, and my best wishes for your speedy recovery."

"Thanks." Trip takes his hand back, rubbing his pinky off on Rudy's jeans. "Now, let's get that gate open. Got a dying man here."

"Jivllrrrle'remmm, open the gate!" Dure'relementrrrrmmm calls, and the gate behind the tree guardian rolls up.

The tree guardian steps to one side, and Trip twitches the *Wound* into drive, waving at Dure'relementrrrrmmm as he has the car start toward the gate. "Sucker," he says under his breath.

"You know, sometimes you can be a real asshole, but I knew, at the end of the day, deep down, you care," Rudy says as the *Wound* eases through the open gate into a paradise of lush greenery. "I may not be dying, but I admit, I could maybe use some medical attention about now. Nice to know I can count on you, brother."

"Yep, count on me."

"We're not really going to the hospital, are we?"

"What do you think?"

"But you made a pinky promise."

"With a tentacle. Ewww. Doesn't count."

CHAPTER SIXTEEN

"WHAT ARE YOU DOING?" one of two Cthulist guards asks, lowering his triple-bladed scythe to block access to the curtain of broad green and purple leaves separating the receiving area and King-Chief Mugatham'mmmrrrrr's council chamber, high atop the tallest tree cluster in the city-state.

"Just trying to get a peek in," Trip says, gently pushing the scythe up and out of his way to peer through a gap in the leaves. The council chamber beyond the curtain is quiet, and empty. Shafts of light appear and vanish, the sun shining through the ceiling, a domed canopy of interwoven tree branches blowing gently in the wind. The floor of the chamber is carpeted in grass, a wide circle of it in the center an inch shorter than the rest, delineating a conference area.

Trip reaches up to part the curtain.

The second guard's hand shoots out, wrapping around Trip's wrist. "Please stand back, human."

"We've been standing back for two hours," Trip says, shrugging out of the guard's grasp. He rubs his wrist. "Now, we stand forward."

Rudy, dabbing sweat from his pallid forehead with a handkerchief, steps up next to Trip. "Yeah, forward," he says, going up on tiptoes to find a crack the look through.

The first guard lets out a hissing grunt. "This is highly irregular."

"I know," Trip says, lighting a cigarette, "but like I told you, the guy at the front gate said it'd be okay."

"There he is," Rudy announces.

Trip throws back the curtain before the guards can stop him. "Hey, Mugatham'mmmmrrrrr, it's me, your old pal Trip!" he calls out at the tall, muscular Cthulist in ornate robes entering the chamber through another curtained archway in the back, flanked by smaller Cthulists in less ornate robes.

"And Rudy!" Rudy shouts out, waving. "Remember me? You came to my wedding?"

Across the chamber, Mugatham'mmmrrrrr looks up. He dismisses his counselors and lopes gracefully across the chamber.

"I will not tell you again, human," the first guard says, slipping in front of Rudy, his scythe between them at the ready. "Stand back."

"Forgive the intrusion, my king," the second guard says, grabbing Trip by both shoulders and standing at attention as Mugatham'mmmmrrrrr approaches. "Rest assured, I will teach these humans respect."

"Rudy? Is that you?" Mugatham'mmmmrrrrr asks, squinting. The Chief-King takes a pair of half-moon glasses from a robe pocket and places them near his chin, where they are grabbed by a half-dozen of his facial tentacles. The tentacles fit the glasses over his nose, holding them in place while he studies the Rudy. "Yes, yes, of course I remember you!" The tentacles lower the glasses and he takes them in his hand, putting them away in his robe. "How good to see you. How are your darling broodlings, and that lovely wife of yours?"

"They're all good," Rudy says, proudly. "Bernice is a militia leader now."

"Oh, how excellent! Do tell her hello for me. And give those kids a big hug from their old uncle Mugatham'mmmrrrrr."

"Will do," Rudy says.

"Umm, hello, still being manhandled here," Trip says, struggling to get out of the guard's iron grip on his shoulders.

"Trip," the King-Chief says with narrowed eyes.

"Mugatham'mmmrrrrr," Trip says with a sardonic smirk.

"You've got a lot of nerve showing your face here."

"This is the fake out bit where you hug me and all is forgiven, right?"

"No, this is where I have you dragged to the prison pit of Gigontua."

"Is it a five-star prison pit?" Trip asks. "Because I only do five-star prison pits."

"Make sure he gets the Presidential suite," Mugatham'mmmrrrrr says to the guard.

"That's better. Wait... that's just a cell with extra-large snakes or something in it, isn't it?"

"Spiders," the guard holding Trip says, his boneless fingers clamping sharply into his shoulders. "Extra extra-large."

"Oh, come on," Trip says.

"You hit on my wife," Mugatham'mmmrrrrr says.

"I hit on a lot of women. Frankly, instead of being offended, I'd think you'd be flattered. And proud. Of her. She didn't hit back."

"She didn't hit back then, no," Mugatham'mmmrrrrr says. "But it got her thinking. About our future. As a couple. She made me do date nights. You believe that? Date nights. No one enjoys painting pottery. And then she started dropping big hints that I maybe shouldn't have so many mistresses."

"Oh."

"Yes, oh. It got so bad I had to send her away on holiday with her mother. And then out of solidarity every single one of my mistresses quit."

"Wait, what?" Trip asks. "You had paid mistresses?"

Mugatham'mmmrrrrr asks, "You don't pay your mistresses?"

"No mistresses at the present... but when I do get one, it's not going to be a paid position."

"But if you don't pay them, how do you get them to sleep with you?"

"Oh, man, Mugatham'mmmrrrrr, buddy, that's so sad," Rudy says.

"But you're king," Trip says. "Isn't that like an automatic panty-dropper? Like, gratis automatic?"

"I am done with this conversation," Mugatham'mmmrrrrr says, abruptly waving at the guard. "Take him away."

"Mugatham'mmmrrrrr, please," Rudy protests as the guard shifts his hold on Trip to under his arms and easily lifts him a few inches off the grass-covered floor. "He's an asshole, but we did come here with good intentions."

"Yeah," Trip says, twisting and turning in the guard's grasp, his fleet flailing as he's carried towards an open-platform elevator. "Awesomely good intentions!"

"What good intentions could you possibly have?" Mugatham'mmmrrrrr asks. "You intend to hit on my daughter?"

Trip's eyebrow goes up. "You have a daughter?"

"Focus, Trip," Rudy says. His nose wriggles as he catches the scent of fruit and pastries from somewhere back in the council chamber. "Is that a snack table?" he asks, wandering off to investigate.

"Right!" Trip yells, the guard dragging him stepping on the elevator. "We're here to stop the war. Gotta admit—that's a pretty good intention, right? Honorable. Noble, even."

"Hold," Mugatham'mmmrrrrr commands the guard. "Why would I want to stop the war?"

"Because it's going to lead to the end of the world."

"But I want the end of the world," Mugatham'mmmrrrrr says. "So the Formless Ones can return and walk over their rightful land."

"But that means you're all going to have to suicide," Trip says. Still dangling in the air in the guard's grasp, Trip crosses his legs and lights a cigarette. "To open the portal or whatever."

"Ritual self-sacrifice to open the Time of Invitation," Mugatham'mmmrrrrr says. "And it will be worth it to ascend to the comets, where our souls can watch the Formless Ones frolic and play on the earth that we prepared for them, free of all lesser beings."

Trip slips his Zippo away and sends smoke rings up at the guard. "Like us."

"We are not worthy to be in the same plane of existence as the Formless Ones," Mugatham'mmmrrrrr says.

"Which kind of is the point I'm getting to."

"You may release him. For now," Mugatham'mmmrrrrr says to the guard. "How so?" he asks Trip as the guard abruptly drops Trip.

Trip stands up, dusting off his tux lapels, and walks back to the Chief-King. "You've got it pretty good here, right. You've got the market on food in the Wasteland covered—you're arguably the more successful, wealthiest, and most comfortable civilization on the planet. And with your network of tribal-states, you're one of the most influential power blocs out there. People respect you.

When the Cthulist speak—when the Cthulists king speaks—people listen."

"They do," Mugatham'mmmrrrrr says. "They do listen."

"Yep. But that all goes away the moment you plunge those sacrificial daggers into your hearts," Trip says, drawing a thumb across the front of his neck. "Who's gonna listen to you once you're a disembodied soul on a comet way out in the middle of nowhere space? Not the Formless Ones. And why would they listen? They're gods, by Shatner. You said it yourself, you're not worthy of them. They're not going to listen—hell, they probably won't even be able to hear you, you'll be so small and insignificant to them."

"You have a point, but it does not matter." Mugatham'mmmr-rrrr spins on his heel and walks out into the council chamber, through the slashes of sunlight. "Our very existence has been leading to this moment... generations of genetic manipulation, this war, it is our destiny."

"Sure, sure," Trip says, following, "but who says it has to be this generation's destiny?"

"What do you mean?"

"Why not kick the can?" Trip says, throwing his arm around Mugatham'mmmrrrrr's shoulders. "Down the road. Let some other sucker generation do the ritual self-sacrificing, while you stick around and continue being a big fish in a small pond. And maybe your kids and their kids can be big fish, too. Something they'll never even get a chance to be if you go all stabby-hearty now."

"It would be nice to see my Bradulithuni'mmmrrrrr on the throne." Mugatham'mmmrrrrr pulls away and steps into the circle of short grass. He lowers himself, sitting cross-legged. "But the Formless Ones... we have an obligation. And the war to end all wars has already begun."

"The Formless Ones have waited this long to come back." Trip plops down onto the short grass in front of Mugatham'mmmrrrrr, stretching himself out prone on his side, propping his head up on his elbow. "They can wait a little more. And it's not like the war is exactly going your way, is it?"

"We're winning."

"Are you?" Trip asks. "From what I see, I see a tie so far. You take a region. The Chinese take a province. And so it goes, back and forth, nobody making any real headway. So it's a stalemate. Nobody's gonna get the upper hand unless you can manage to convince a lot more people to convert and grow your army, which, you gotta admit, is a long shot, especially when the reward for signing up is eventual suicide. Face it, the Chinese don't have that kind of PR problem. The only thing holding them back is the logistics of getting troops from the mainland over here faster. But they'll have that licked soon enough — once they get the land-bridge over the Aleutians done, they can march billions over here and swamp you practically overnight."

"That has been a concern. But we are working on counter-measures."

"You can weaponize all the trees you want, but at the end of the day, you've got a billion plus Chinese coming for you. Not to mention the Indians — you heard the rumors coming out of Mumbai, right? They're about ready to settle their differences with the Chinese and join the fight against the gene-freaks. Their words."

Mugatham'mmmrrrr shakes his head, his chin-tentacles flopping from side to side. "The Indians would never deal with the Chinese. Not after what they did to Visakhapatnam."

"I think you underestimate the fear and loathing you guys and your agenda inspire. Wouldn't surprise me to see the world uniting against you the second it seems like the tide is turning in your favor. Nobody but you wants to see the world end. At least not in a forced mass suicide."

"We won't lose the war." Mugatham'mmmrrrrr raises his hands to the ceiling. "We have the gods on our side."

"Said every loser ever. And then what happens to the Formless Ones' dream of coming back? It could be a thousand years or more before you're strong enough to spark a final war again. And that's assuming the rest of the world leaves any of you alive to get the chance."

Mugatham'mmmrrrrr's hands drop to his side. "You know, I told Bradulithuni'mmmrrrrr going to war now was a mistake. We needed more time to build our forces, to ensure a victory." The Cthulist's blood red eyes look sadly at Trip. "We need to make peace."

Trip nods. "You need to make peace."

"But how? We're so entrenched... and the Chinese are bent on completing their occupation. If we unilaterally pull back they'll simply sweep over us."

Trip sits up, flicking his cig to the side. "That's where I come in."

"You?"

"I'll talk to them."

"To the Chinese?"

"Yeah."

"Why would they listen to you?"

"I'm charming," Trip says with a broad smile. "Talked to you for two minutes and got you to want peace, didn't I?"

Mugatham'mmmrrrrr frowns. "I'm assuming because you are you, there will be a fee for this service?"

"Oh, yeah. Big one. But split between all the warring parties, so the individual contributions won't be that bad." Trip thrusts his hand out. "We got a deal?"

Mugatham'mmmrrrrr's hand slowly stretches out towards Trip's. "We have a—"

The Chief-King is interrupted as a Cthulist in a plain yellow robe with a jagged scar across her forehead bursts through the curtain to the receiving room.

"Sir!" the Cthulist announces, catching her breath. "An aircraft has landed in the courtyard!"

"An aircraft?" Mugatham'mmmrrrrr asks, bemused. "No dirigible can penetrate our air defenses."

"And no dirigible has," says the golden-skinned woman in a leather aviator's jacket, a billowing white silk scarf flapping behind her, as she pushes through the curtains and past the Cthulist in the yellow robe. "I came by jet. Jet plane. Outflew your anti-dirigible guns like they weren't there."

"Lock," Trip says, shaking his head in disbelief.

"You know this woman?" Mugatham'mmmrrrrr asks.

"She's sorta my daughter," Trip says. He lights a cig. "And hence, she's not to be trusted. Or listened to. In fact, you're better off just shooing her off now without letting her speak."

"Is this true?" Mugatham'mmmrrrrr asks, getting to his feet. "You came here in a jet... *plane?*"

"It's outside." Lock yanks off her gloves. "And there's more where it came from. I'm taking pre-orders now."

Trip hastily stands. "Mugatham'mmmrrrrr, about our plan... a peaceful end to the war, remember? If we could just shake on it..."

"Um, later. Later," Mugatham'mmmrrrrr says, ignoring the offered hand. "Right now, I want to see this plane of yours, Lock. How much did you say they were? And how many can you get me?"

CHAPTER SEVENTEEN

"WELL, that was a little bit of bad luck," Rudy says. He's standing in front of the *Wound*, parked on a grassy knoll a few miles down the road from the Cthulist enclave, chewing on a pear, watching the wind take the contrails Lock's jet left behind when she flew overhead a few seconds ago, a sonic boom announcing her departure.

Trip sits cross-legged on the hood of the *Wound*, his eyes closed. "Yep."

"Nice jet, though." Rudy takes a big bite of pear. The fruit, and the warm sun, have got him feeling better about his forced detox. At least he's not sweating as much anymore, and his skin is almost back to its usual ruddy pallor. "She's gonna sell a million of them."

"If not more," Trip says flatly.

"I wonder how many Mugatham'mmmrrrrr bought."

"As many as he could, I reckon."

"So, what now?" Rudy asks. "We try the Chinese?"

"No point."

"Oh, because Hu hates your guts and would sooner beat you to death with her shiny new peg leg than talk to you, especially after that mauling she took at the start of the war?"

"No, because that's where Lock is headed now. What inventory Mugatham'mmmrrrrr didn't buy, the Chinese will."

"So, diplomacy's a no-go?"

"That window has closed."

"Then how do we stop the war?" Rudy turns to look at his brother. "You do still want to stop the war, right?"

"I do, and will," Trip says, without opening his eyes.

"How?"

"I have no idea," Trip answers, and reaches up behind his left ear to flick a small control nub underneath his blinking antenna, plunging him into real darkness.

A moment later. Or maybe a year.

Trip's breathing steadies, and in his mind's cybernetic-implant eye, with a flash of static washing over his consciousness, he sees stretching out before him a vast land of barely restrained chaos. It's a churning vista of data, below a sea of bits, fragments of command and control code bobbing in it like icebergs, and above a sky of data streams, intra-system communiqués flashing through it like lightning.

And at its center, a black box. Light years across, but also smaller than a hair's breadth. It sits there, doing nothing, being nothing, but somehow also being the center of this little pocket universe of data.

As so far, impenetrable.

He's poked it a thousand times, from a million different angles, and nothing. No response, no reaction. It might as well be a dead part of the implant, and when he'd found it that first time, that's exactly what he thought it was, some part of the centuries-old alien biomechanical matrix that had simply given out, no longer able to repair itself thanks to old age, unable to hold data or process information. But if was simply the manifestation of dead tissue, why was it exactly square on all sides instead of jagged and random like he would have expected? And why would the manifestation of dead tissue have, inscribed identically on each facet, a smirking smiling face... his face?

So, not dead tissue.

A memory bank, then. But a protected one, not in the implant's main line, inaccessible without a key, or maybe not at all. Holding something. Something from long ago. Something an ancestor had squirreled away for safekeeping. Something of such earth-shattering importance that it must be protected, sustained over the generations, hidden and secret. Or so he'd come to assume, building it up over time. It could, for all he knows, just as easily contain a not particularly special recipe for an Old Fashioned.

But whatever it is, his curiosity was piqued, and he has to know. Today's gonna be the day. Has to be.

He could use a win about now.

He sends out a probe. And another. And another, and another, and another. A thousand data tendrils, one after the other, and sometimes all together, thwacking against the sides of the big black box, feeling for any weakness, any soft spot, that can then be ripped into an opening.

And as always happens his thoughts begin to drift.

So Lock cracked the secret to avoiding Death From Above. So what? She's a smart kid. And she's got those nanochines. If I had those nanochines, I'd have cracked it, too. And faster, you can bet your ass about that.

Still, nothing. Each probe bounces off, the walls of the black box as strong as ever.

Trip sends another wave of probes—twice as many and twice as fast as he ever has, all at the same time.

And Rox... I'm happy for her. Okay, maybe not happy. But not angry. No, not angry. Never angry. Jealous, maybe. What? Me, jealous? Ha. Never. Okay, it's just you and me here, and you're me. Maybe a little. Just a little. So little I'd never have to admit it to her. That's almost like I'm not jealous at all, right? I mean, for all practical purposes.

The massive wave of tendril probes crash against the monolithic box, pummeling it until the last probe disintegrates into data dust. And when the dust clears, the box remains, its walls intact, his own stupid grinning face taunting him.

But can you blame me? She took my job. And she's better at it. Way better. She actually cares about that shit-hole of a town. Cares about me. Cares enough to have my kid. My kid. A kid... Vishnu's nipples, I'm gonna be a daddy...

With a warbling war-cry, Trip sends his consciousness spiraling up, up into the clouds of data, up past the binary lightning storms, past the blinking stars, pinpricks of memories, his, his ancestors', everyone who'd ever worn the implant, and then down, back down, his consciousness constricting, forcing all his speed into the fall, faster and faster, a bullet aimed straight at the top of the cube, right at the center of that mocking asshole's smirk.

How fucked up is that?

The big black box rushing up at him at ever increasing speed, his own face getting larger and larger and larger, miles away, meters, inches... Trip steals himself for the impact.

The blow never comes. Only darkness.

It seems to go on forever. Swallows him whole. Never-ending. Pressing in on him. A nothingness. Void.

This is it. I've gone and done it now. Broke the damn implant. And maybe my brain, too. Nice job, asshole.

"Stop being so dramatic."

And then...

Light.

CHAPTER EIGHTEEN

THE VIRTUAL REALITY that coalesces around Trip is both foreign, yet familiar.

He's seen it before, this sharply appointed space, with its curving walls, twin couches facing each other across a big blue rug with some kind of militarized bird on it, a bust broken into dark gray blocks and dust at the base of a side table, and floor-to-ceiling windows behind a dark wood desk.

But Trip's damn sure he's never seen it before with his eyes.

No, not his eyes.

That other him. His eyes.

The one in the black sports jacket, skinny tie, and jeans, sitting at that desk, leaning back, his feet up, red Converses on the desk, puffing away smugly at a cigar, and smirking at Trip.

But it's not Trip there behind the desk. The shoulders are wrong. Broader. And there's gray at this other Trip's temples. And maybe a few wrinkles around his eyes.

Age, yeah. This Trip's older. But that's not what's ever so slightly off about him.

"You're not me," Trip says.

"And it only took you how long to figure that out?" the man behind the desk says. "I mean, I assumed it was only going to go downhill from me, but gotta say, that's still surprising."

Trip snaps his fingers. "I know you. You're the first. To wear the implant. My great-great-great-great grandfather—"

"No names," the man says. "You never know who might be listening."

"And I know this room. How do I know this room?"

Granpap swings his feet off the desk. "For a time, it was the office of the most powerful man in the world. Like between '45 and '73, '74. Then corporate interests took over behind the scenes, like Ike warned everybody about, and then it was just the office of a series of increasingly ineffective corporate stooges, until the Wultr came along, bought the planet's debt, and gave the office to somebody who knew how to do some serious business."

"You?"

"You want a history lesson or do you want my help?"

"Help?"

"That's why I put a version of myself in here, in the implant." Granpap taps the side of his head with a middle finger. "To help future generations. Which, it appears I assumed rightly, would need all the help they could get."

"I thought you were a treasure map or something."

"Well, I'm not. What I am is something a lot more valuable. Like, sum total of experience and wisdom of our bloodline's greatest generation valuable — the mind and memories of the peak iteration, at your service, and at an unprecedented price. Free. You can't beat that."

"I do all right on my own, thank you," Trip says. "So if it's all the same to you, I'd rather have a treasure map."

"Right, right. Doing great on your own." Granpap taps ashes

into a large glass bowl. "You even bother to ask yourself why now?"

"Why what now?"

"Why did you become aware of my memory bubble just a couple months back when I've been here all along? And why, after so many attempts to break in did you finally manage it? What's so special? What was the key?"

"Persistence?"

"Self-doubt."

Trip huffs. "Yeah, right."

"You can hide it from yourself, but not me. This implant of ours, it sees deeper into the brain than you know—than you can even be aware of. The Wultr were horrible businessmen, and boy could they run a planet into the ground, but they knew how to salvage, and the aliens they salvaged these implants from, they knew their shit. Thanks to this thing, I know you better than you know yourself, and I'm a fuckin' ghost. I see everything in here. Every little thought. And for the first time in your life, you've been feeling self-doubt. A little at first, but it built and built over the months, until *pow!* It was like an earthquake down here. You see that bust. That wasn't on the floor in pieces five minutes ago. So don't deny it."

Trip plops down onto one of the couches, leaning forward, elbow on knees. "Okay, sure, maybe I've felt a tinge of doubt here and there, but I've never been a dad before. A real dad. One with a little baby that's going to depend on me. I can't even stop a war, how am I supposed to raise a kid—"

Granpap interrupts. "Enough with the soul-searching introspective bullshit, already. Snap out of it. I won't have any ancestor of mine tainting my legacy with self-doubt."

"Fuck you."

"Better," Granpap says with a smile. "Now, if I tell you how to stop this war of yours, you think you can stop being a wittle baby?"

"How do I stop the war? I don't have an army."

"You don't need an army. First, you got to get yourself off planet."

"Get my ass to Mars, eh?" Trip asks in a growly, weirdly accented voice.

"You can reference a two-hundred year old movie but you don't recognize the Oval Office?" Granpap shakes his head. "No, not to Mars. I've been. Horrible pizza. Anyway, after what me and Davey did to the place, doubt you'd be welcome. Just get yourself into orbit. Then we'll go from there."

"Orbit? Funny... that would have been impossible up to about twenty minutes ago."

"You think that's a coincidence?" Granpap stabs his cigar out in the ashtray. "You're not the only head I'm in."

"You're in Lock?" Trip asks, lighting a cig of his own.

"An echo. She doesn't have an implant, but she does have nanomachine memory cells. Open-standard, open-source ones. When you interfaced with her while she was the All-Mart, I managed to copy myself over into her."

"She know you're in there?"

"Not consciously. Yet. She's pretty bright. Brighter than you. I'm sure she'll detect my influence someday."

Trip looks up. "Wait... how much of her deciding to give up being the All-Mart was you?"

"That was all her. But her not killing Rox... that was pretty much all me."

"Ah."

"Yeah, don't trust her."

CHAPTER NINETEEN

"YOU SURE you're up for this?" Trip asks, crouched behind a crate and peering around it to look out at the tarmac on the south end of the Combine.

"I'm sure," Rudy says, crouched right behind him, looking up at the moon, a crescent in the inky black sky, gnawing on a stalk of some green-red leafy thing.

Trip looks back at him over his shoulder. "I don't need your detoxing ass fucking this up. We may only get the one chance."

"Never been better," Rudy says, grinning around a mouthful of leaf.

"Well, you look like hell. And not your normal third level of hell but like level six and a half."

"Is that the one with the vampire bats?"

"And a rerun of the musical Lexx episode on a loop projected on every wall."

"I'm fine, really," Rudy says. "The detox cycle is almost done and I'm feeling good. Better than good. Ready to take on the world."

"Really? Because you still seem to be sweating a lot, is all I'm saying. And your pupils are dilated. And your hand seems to be shaking quite a bit. And there's blood coming out of your nose."

"Only a trickle. Look, don't worry about it, it's just the gonka."

"Is that what that is? I thought it was lettuce."

"It ain't lettuce." Rudy tears a chunk of the gonka off with his teeth with the gusto of a man biting into a perfectly rare dry-aged steak. "Got it from the Cthulists. And it's amazing. It's really taking the edge off the whole detox thing. Now, what's the plan?"

"Seriously? We went over the plan like a thousand times on the drive over here."

"Oh, my bad." Rudy shrugs. "So what's the plan, again?"

"Vishnu's Interocitor, dude," Trip says, exasperated. "I'm just gonna steal the jet myself."

"No, no, I'm onboard. I can focus. Swear."

Trip reaches for Rudy's gonka. "Okay, but no more gonka—"

Rudy pulls the gonka back, close to his chest, and snarls. "You did not just try to touch my gonka, did you?"

"Settle down, someone might hear you."

"It's the middle of the night, who's gonna hear us?"

"Lock's not dumb." Trip jogs his head towards the man lying unconscious on the tarmac nearby, the one he'd snuck up behind and stun-gunned a few moments earlier. "There will be other sentries."

Rudy looks over at the prone sentry. "Sure I can't draw a mustache on him?"

"Don't you think I'd love to draw some handlebars on him? No, we need to focus."

"You're right. Focus." Rudy pulls a nub of charcoal out of his bandolier. "I'm just gonna draw a small one on him."

Trip knocks the charcoal out of Rudy's hand. "Just eat your gonka and pay attention. Think you can do that?"

"Yeah, I guess," Rudy says, a touch of sadness in his voice. "But when that guy wakes up without a charcoal Van Dyke, that's on you, brother."

"Okay, maybe just a small one," Trip says, glancing around them. "But be quick about it."

"On it." Rudy grabs the charcoal from the tarmac and, still couching, waddles over to the sentry. "Now tell me the plan."

"I'll wait until I have your full attention."

Rudy rolls the sentry over onto his back and starts in on drawing. "Let's face it, you are never going to have my full attention. But thanks to the gonka, I'm feeling fairly confident I can do two things at once. Maybe even three — if you count chewing the gonka. Man, gonka is amazing. Now, be honest with me. Are my ears bleeding?"

"Yes, yes they are."

"Whew, that's a relief, I thought I was hallucinating again," Rudy says, tearing off more of the gonka. "Okay, hit me up with the plan."

"First, we sneak into Lock's city under cover of darkness."

"Done," Rudy says, dabbing a final touch of charcoal on the sentry's chin. "And done."

"Then we find the prototype jet."

"Which I'm guessing is that thing of beauty over there," Rudy says, nodding at the small twin-engine jet sitting on the tarmac a few hundred paces away.

"Right." Trip glances around them one last time to check the shadows for other sentries. "Come on, let's go. Time to steal it," he says, standing and heading not for the jet, but a portable staircase on wheels near it.

Rudy rushes to catch up with him. "Wait, what about the rest of the plan?"

"We steal the jet, I figure out how to interface with it, then we fly it into orbit."

"Into orbit?"

"Yes, into orbit," Trip says, grabbing the staircase and pushing it towards the jet. "We've gone over this."

"Yeah, but... can the jet get into orbit?"

Trip eases the staircase up against the jet's canopy with a soft thud as the staircase bumps against the fuselage. "I don't know. It's a scramjet. The ghost in my head seems to think it can."

"Oh, right. Virtual great-great-grandpappy. When do I get to meet him? I've got so many questions about the past... like, why did they let Zach Snyder keep making DC movies?"

"I don't think it works that way." Trip lights a cig, stepping on the first stair. "He's my ghost, tied to my implant, I don't know if he can come out and play. Besides, he's a bit of an asshole."

"Like I'm not used to hanging out with assholes."

"Shut up and keep an eye out for sentries." Trip gingerly mounts the stairs, trying to make as little sound as he can. His footsteps still clang with every step, and the staircase creaks with his weight. At the top, looking down through the canopy, he says, "Oh..."

"What?"

"There's only the one seat. And before you ask, no, we're not doubling up. Looks like it's going to be a solo flight."

"Shit, I wanted to go into space, too."

"You can take her for a spin after I come back."

"Right, like you're coming back."

"What's that supposed to mean?" Trip asks, flicking the exterior latches to raise the canopy. "You saw Lock fly it, Death From Above won't touch it."

"I'm not talking about Death From Above. Come on, we both know this is just one of your elaborate misdirections. You're just stealing the jet to run farther away this time, somewhere Rox can't track you down easily."

"It's not a misdirection," Trip says, bending down to get a better look at the cockpit. "I swear."

"Yeah, a ghost in your head wants you to steal a jet so you can get into orbit. Which will somehow let you stop the war. Right."

"I don't know which is more insulting. The idea that you think I'm running away, or the idea that you don't think I can come up with a better misdirection." Trip straightens and sighs. "Shatner... I can't find an interface. Nowhere to plug in, and no wireless connection point I can sense. And no manual flight controls, either."

"That's because there aren't any," a familiar voice says from below.

"Oh, hey," Rudy announces. "Trip, Lock's here."

Trip looks down. Lock stands at the base of the staircase, fists planted against her hips. "I can see that," Trip says.

"Snuck up on me," Rudy says.

"How about you stick to one thing at a time from here on in, gonka regardless?" Trip suggests to Rudy, then smirks at Lock. "What do you mean there's no interface? How are people gonna fly it?"

"It's a prototype. The production model will have flight controls. This one I fly by nano-connection," Lock says, waving her fingers in front of her face, fingertips giving off a cloud of microscopic machines.

"Well, do some nano-magic and reconfigure it to have a neural interface," Trip says. He looks around the tarmac, past the crates they were hiding behind, and into the shadows of the hangar beyond. *If Lock came with backup, they're hiding real well.* "Gotta borrow it."

"Not a good idea."

"You gonna try and stop me?"

"Don't need to," Lock says. "Death From Above will."

Trip thumps the side of the jet with his palm. "This thing flies. We saw it. Didn't get blown away."

"Sure, because I was aboard," Lock says.

"Of course," Trip says. "That's how you licked the problem. By not licking it."

"I'm missing something," Rudy says.

"Usually," Trip says. "She cheated."

"Not cheated," Lock says. "Just needed a working prototype. And fast. The Belgians are on the verge of a breakthrough."

"So you faked having a solution so you can get enough pre-orders to pay for coming up with a real solution," Trip says.

"And divert any potential orders from the Belgians. Fuck them."

"Wait, but we saw it fly. That wasn't fake. Or was it? Was it some kind of hologram?" Rudy shoves a handful of gonka into his mouth. "It was a hologram, wasn't it?" he asks, chewing.

"Not a hologram," Trip says. He smirks at Lock. "You were in that jet, and it flew. So how'd you pull it off?"

"I cover the thing in a sheath of nanomachines I extrude. I figured if I could keep the nanomachines in motion, a constant shift between ablative and nonablative, deflecting and absorbing electromagnetic spectrum randomly, it would continually mask the thing from Death From Above's sensors."

"It worked," Trip says.

"Sure did. Only thing is, my nanomachines have enough CPU of their own to do simple tasks, but they don't have enough onboard computer power to keep up with the processing needed to keep the jet masked, even when they're networked together."

"They need your core processor."

"It takes most of my concentration to do it. And it means I

have to be in physical contact with them—bandwidth of our link isn't fat enough or fast enough to do it over the wireless."

"So you can't just detach a bunch of them and sell them along with the jets. Without you, they'd have no computer to do the magic."

"It's not just that. I only have so many nanomachines. Sure, they self-repair, and I can make new ones, over time, but not quickly. Not anywhere quick enough. It takes about five percent of my mass to make the masking sheath, and a year for me to produce that much new nanomachine mass."

"So even if you had a computer to go with them, you could sell maybe nineteen jets before—"

"Before it became impractical, yeah," Lock says. "So I need to find another way. Some way that doesn't depend on my nanomachines. Or at least not so many of them. And it also means, if you're looking to steal the jet to reverse engineer it, you're out of luck, there, dad."

"Not reverse-engineering. And not stealing. I told you. I'm borrowing. I'll bring it back."

Lock looks at him dubiously. "Borrowing it why?"

"He needs to get into orbit," Rudy says.

"Orbit?" Lock asks. "Why do you need to get into orbit?"

"I have no idea," Trip says.

"The ghost hasn't told him yet," Rudy says, Trip shooting him an unhappy glare that he mentioned Granpap. "If the ghost actually exists," Rudy quickly adds.

"The ghost?" Lock asks.

"Some kind of digital revenant in his implant," Rudy says, getting another unhappy glare.

Lock sucks in a deep breath and nods. "Should have guessed you'd have a copy of him in you, too."

"You know about your ghost?" Trip asks.

"He's not as clever as he thinks he is," Lock says. "None of your ancestors were."

"Clever enough to survive for a couple hundred years hidden through the generations," Trip says. "Which makes me curious about him. And his motives. Aren't you curious about why he wants me to get into orbit?"

"Maybe a little."

"Then come with me and find out."

"You mean come with us," Rudy says.

Trip snorts. "Us?"

"I wanna see space," Rudy insists.

"Okay, fine, but that gonka crap is staying here. Don't need it stinking up the cabin."

"You're jumping the gun, Trip," Lock says. "I haven't agreed to come."

"Of course you did. You wouldn't be here if you hadn't already made the decision."

Lock shrugs. "We're going to need a bigger jet."

CHAPTER TWENTY

"I WANNA SAY *WOO-HOO,*" Rudy says from behind a pressure mask, as scram-jets light, kicking the spaceplane over another sound barrier. "Can I say *woo-hoo?*"

"Knock yourself out," Lock replies back over her pressure mask's built-in mic. Eyes gone over to blinking green, her hands extended towards the featureless dashboard, her fingers wriggle, swirling clouds of nanomachines trailing around her fingertips.

The real clouds fall away beneath them and Rudy lets out a whoop.

"Sure this thing isn't going to fall apart?" Trip asks, looking out the wide canopy at the port delta wing. He swears he can see it shaking, flapping up and down like a bird's wing. "It feels like it's going to fall apart."

"That's just turbulence," Lock says. "It'll settle down once we hit the ionosphere."

Trip grips the armrests of his acceleration couch tighter and he stares straight ahead. "Nobody said anything about turbulence."

Lock glances back at him. "This was your idea, remember?"

"Last time I listen to a digital artifact," Trip says. "And last time I let somebody else drive."

"Hold on, I'll tweak the flight surface shape. That might help." Lock lets out a chuckle. "If you can't take a little harmless shimmy."

"Don't worry about it," Trip says. "Just concentrate on keeping the nanomachine sheath working."

"We haven't been blown out of the sky yet, have we?"

"We're not in orbit yet."

"Speaking of which, any word from the ghost about what we're supposed to do when we get there?" Rudy asks.

"He's not the talkative type." Trip closes his eyes and taps the nub behind his ear. "Let me check in."

The old man's lying on one of the couches when Trip pops into the Oval Office this time, wrapped up in a colorful Afghan, snoring.

He comes awake with a snort. "What, you again?"

"Okay, granpap, we're almost in orbit," Trip says, plopping down onto the other couch. "What's next?"

Grandpap sits up. Under the Afghan he's wearing long-sleeved pajamas with a galloping horse pattern. "You actually made it to orbit?"

"Just about, yeah. Any second now. Why is that so surprising?"

"You're no me. Plus you've got that anchor Rudy around your ankle."

"Look, he may be an anchor, but he's still my brother. And you know, I can live without the implant, so let's try and be a little less awful, all right? What's next after we reach orbit?"

"It's not obvious? Even to you?"

"Let's say for the sake of argument that it's not and just tell me already."

"Why am I even bothering to help you?"

"Would you rather I bring Rudy in here so you can work with him instead of me?"

"Okay, here's the plan..."

Trip opens his eyes and sees the Earth filling the canopy, a sparkling blue-white curve of Pacific Ocean filling the horizon. The only sound in the suddenly not shaking cockpit is the sound of his own breath inside his pressure mask.

"We made orbit?" Trip asks, his voice coming out in an awed whisper.

Rudy, staring out the canopy, his jaw slack under his own pressure mask, eyes wide, can only nod.

"We are in orbit," Lock says, tearing her gaze away from the vista before them. "I've reconfigured the jet into an orbital vehicle while we wait for instruction. Do we have instruction?"

"We do," Trip says, watching the Earth slide by below them. "Can you reconfigure the jet to get us into high geo-synch orbit?"

Lock thinks for a moment. "Sure." Her fingers wave at the dashboard and around them, the spaceplane starts creaking, cracking, and humming, its parts being reshaped by nanochine constructors. "Where after this?"

"Inside Death From Above," Trip says.

"He wants us to go inside a space dragon?" Rudy asks.

"Death From Above ain't no space dragon," Trip says. "What makes you think it's a space dragon?"

"That's what people say."

"And that made sense to you?"

"I'm stoned. All the time. Of course it made sense to me."

"Point," Trip says. "But according to the ghost, Death From Above is really a web of over four hundred space-based high-energy pulse gun-equipped sats, networked together, all in geo-synch orbit watching day and night."

"I guess that does make more sense than space dragons," Rudy admits grudgingly. "Except why would sats flame out everything that flies? I mean, I can see dragons doing it, you know, being the envious and petty creatures they are, but sats? What do they have to be jealous about?"

"Flaming anything that flies wasn't what it was originally designed for," Trip says. "It was launched after the Wultr were forced off planet, part of a scheme to protect Earth from future alien invasions."

"If it was designed to repel aliens, it's shooting in the wrong direction," Lock says.

"Blame low-bid government contracts for that," Trip says. "Shortly after the system went online, the badly programmed AI system controlling the thing suffered a catastrophic system failure and went schizophrenic."

"Typical of AIs of that era," Lock says.

"You're an AI of that era," Trip notes.

"And look how I turned out."

"Yep," Trip says with a smirk. "Instead of shooting at threats from space, it decided the real threat was below, effectively throwing the planet back to the 19th century."

"Why didn't they just shut the AI down?" Rudy asks.

"I imagine they would have," Trip says, "if it was on Earth."

Lock is surprised. "They put the AI in orbit with Death From Above?"

"Where else?" Rudy asks.

"I don't know," Lock says. "Somewhere on Earth where they

could, if everything went to shit and nothing else worked, blow it to bits if it misbehaved."

"I'm beginning to think our ancestors were uniformly dumb," Trip says. "So, yeah, they couldn't shut it off because they couldn't get to it. Couldn't even send a rocket up to take out the control hub."

"Because it would shoot down anything they sent up," Rudy says. "Why not blow the sats up with pulse guns from the surface?"

"Maybe they tried, I dunno," Trip says. "The world can't have been in that great a shape at the time—the Wultr stripped the planet of most everything valuable and the geo-political climate must have been a mess in the wake of their getting the boot. I'm surprised whatever governments were left were able to get their international cooperation on long enough to get the Death From Above system into orbit, let alone take it down once the added chaos of no flight kicked in. Doesn't matter, we just need to get inside."

The sounds of reconfiguration taper off. "Jet's ready," Lock announces.

Trip points out the canopy, at a circle of dull light. "Head there, for the primary gun sat. It's got a command and control temporary habitation hub in it, for manned system inspection visits."

Lock waves a finger at the dashboard and universal thrusters fire briefly, orienting the craft towards the sat. Another flick of her finger and the primary thrusters light. "I wouldn't mind know what we're planning on doing once we get inside."

Trip yanks his pressure mask down around his neck and lights a cig. "Neither would I."

CHAPTER TWENTY-ONE

"WHO DOESN'T LOCK their front door?" Trip asks, pushing off from the spaceplane's cockpit and down through the short connecting tube attached to the gun sat's primary airlock.

Waiting in the airlock, Lock watches as Trip sails on by, crashing into the inner airlock hatch and bumping his head, his cig popping out of his lips and spinning away. "They probably never figured on anyone coming up here unless they were government."

"They had corps back then," Rudy says, slowly floating into the airlock, using handholds built in to the tube to pull himself along. "And private spaceflight."

Trip does a half flip to orient himself across from Lock, and rubs his head. "Maybe the governments weren't worried about it. Like, the system was supposed to be for the benefit of the whole planet, who'd be dumb enough to try and break in and screw with it?"

"Or maybe our ancestors were really just plain idiots," Rudy says, pulling the outer hatch closed behind him. He yanks down the lever inset into the hatch, sealing it up. The airlock's lights go from red to neutral amber.

"Evidence keeps mounting for that, doesn't it?" Lock says, reaching for the inner airlock's lever.

Trip reaches for Lock's wrist, to stop her. Not at all used to moving in microgravity and not holding onto anything to keep him anchored, he misses, sending his whole body tumbling. "We gonna have air on the other side?" he asks, flailing to stop his tumble.

"I'll be fine," Lock says, and yanks down the lever.

"Funny," Trip says, quickly sucking in a breath and clamping his mouth shut, pinching his nose with his thumb and forefinger.

The inner airlock hatch swings open with a hiss of escaping air, dust swirling around them, revealing the spherical room on the other side. Rings of light flicker on inside the room, and from somewhere deep in the walls there's the stuttering whine of an exchanger whirring on.

After a second, Trip stops holding his breath and takes a cautious sniff as he continues to tumble. "Stale. But I'm not dying."

"Okay, we're in," Rudy says, throwing his arms above his head and pushing through the airlock like's he's flying. "Now what?"

"Now we take control of the sat network." Lock says, sending out hair-thin tentacles of nanochines from her fingertips to grab onto surfaces inside the room to pull her through the airlock after Rudy. "Right?"

Trip grabs the side of the airlock to stop his tumbling and pulls himself through. The spherical hub is maybe twenty-five feet in radius, its curving walls stuffed with equipment lockers and sleeping sacks. "I guess."

"It is the obvious thing to do," Lock says.

"You got another plan?" Rudy asks. "What's ghost gramps got to say?"

"Let me check in," Trip says, his hand reaching for the nub behind his ear.

"You do that." Rudy pulls himself along the wall and slips into a sleeping sack. His hand goes up inside his T-shirt to tweak his nipple. "I'm gonna get stoned. In space! How awesome is that?"

"Okay, gramps," Trip says before the office finishes coalescing in his consciousness. "You told me to get to the sat, I'm here. What's next?"

Grandpap steps out of a door concealed in the wall, zipping up his fly as a toilette flushes in the dark behind him. "We take control of the sat network."

"Ah, the obvious thing," Trip says.

"It's not going to be simple." Granpap wags a finger at Trip. "Far beyond your capabilities. I'll have to do it."

"I have picked a few locks in my time, you know."

"You've never picked anything like this. It's an AI. And a crazy one, to boot."

"Speaking as a crazy AI," a new voice says, "we can be tricky."

"Lock?" Trip asks, spinning around to see Lock sitting at the big desk, her feet up on it. "How'd you get in here?"

"*Pfft*," Lock says with a shrug. "There's no real trick to it. Your encryption protocols are a joke."

"They really are, aren't they?" Granpap says, walking over to the desk and sitting down on its edge. "Always was a weak spot with the device."

"You could have fixed it back when you were wearing it," Trip notes.

"Could have, but that would have made ghosting it harder." Granpap smiles at Lock. "You ready?"

"It's why I'm here, isn't it?"

"For a start."

"You have plans?"

"Big ones," Granpap says, and jogs his head at the concealed door to the bathroom. He gets up. "Come on, I'll tell you all about them."

"Wait, where are you two going?" Trip asks.

"To solve your little war problem," Granpap says, opening the bathroom door. On the other side, there's no toilet anymore. Just light.

Lock swings her feet off the big desk and walks towards the light. "And then—"

Granpap interrupts. "No need to worry him about that."

"But that's half the fun," Lock says with an exaggerated frown, "making him worry."

"Go on," Granpap says, gently nudging Lock into the light.

"Wait, you are not really telling me I'm superfluous here, are you?" Trip asks as Lock fades away.

"Good, you figured it out," Granpap says, a silhouette framed against the overwhelming light. "I was afraid I'd have to explain it and embarrass you."

"So what am I supposed to do?"

"Go get stoned with your brother. We've got work to do."

"This stuff is terrible," Trip says. Secured against the gunsat wall by looping a leg through a handrail, he's holding a half-filled sippy-cup near his face and sneering at it. He rubs his lips with the back of his hand, trying to get the rancid taste out of his mouth. "Really."

Hanging next to him in a sleep sack, Rudy shrugs. "You get used to the aftertaste."

"I will never get used to spit," Trip says, giving Rudy the cup.

"Nice buzz, though, right?"

"I feel like somebody over-inflated a balloon in my nasal cavity, and my ears are ringing. Are they supposed to be ringing?"

"Sounds like what you need is more," Rudy says, spitting into the cup through the straw. He hands it back to Trip, gesturing with the cup as he does at Lock, immobile and unresponsive, her palm pressed against a computer interface jack set into the opposite wall. "So, what you think they're doing in there?"

"Who knows?" Trip asks, taking a long suck from the cup. "Who cares?"

Rudy smiles. "See, you are starting to feel it."

"And that's done," Lock announces, moving again.

"What's done?" Trip asks.

Lock takes her palm away from the jack. "War's over."

"What? How?" Trip asks. "It's only been like ten minutes."

"That long? Seemed shorter. Oh, well, I guess time does fly when you're having a ball. Anyway, once we cracked through the AI and replaced it with a copy of me, it was just a matter of taking out a dozen or so strategic HQs and bases on each side, then using the laser network to burn a warning into the moon."

A video screen above the jack turns on. Lock smiles out from the screen. "They got the message, real quick."

"You left your copy in there?" Trip asks.

Granpap appears on the screen next to Lock. "She's not the only copy staying."

"Well, not staying, exactly," the Lock on the screen says.

"What's that supposed to mean?" Trip asks.

"Now that the planet's large-scale-war free for the foreseeable future, time somebody started exploring the galaxy again," Granpap says. "See what's left out there."

"And we're just the AIs to do it," Screen Lock says.

"How are you going to explore when you're stuck inside the sat?" Trip asks.

"I'm leaving them a tenth of my nanochines," Lock says, "to build a probe."

"A probe to go where?"

"There are hints in the sat's databanks of a doomsday cache squirreled away somewhere on the moon," Granpap says. "Ships, nanogenerators, all the fun stuff we need to get started."

"There may even be an intersystem travel engine," Screen Lock says. "I'd love to meet some aliens."

"Just don't piss 'em off," Rudy says.

"Not making any promises."

"Okay," Trip says, taking a sip of spit, "so, you guys are leaving, what happens to Death From Above?"

"We'll leave limited copies of ourselves in here," Granpap says. "Death From Above will remain operational and continue to discourage flight."

"We thought it best," Screen Lock says.

Granpap nods. "Letting you bozos have flight will only bring more tragedy."

"Huh... like you been reading my mind," Trip says with a strong note of contempt. "But a lot of people are close. Lock figured it out, someone else will, soonish."

"We've tweaked the operational parameters, taught the detection system a few thousand new computational tricks," Granpap says. "Nothing anybody on Earth will come up with in the next hundred years will be able to circumvent the restriction."

"And that includes nanosheaths." Screen Lock smiles. "Nobody's flying again, for a very long time."

"Wait a minute," Rudy says. "The nanosheath's our only way home."

"We'll be staying until you're planetside," Granpap says. "We'll keep the network from blowing you away."

"It'll take that long to build the probe and figure out where the cache is, anyway," Screen Lock says.

"But then we're stuck?" Trip asks. "On earth?"

"Until we get back," Granpap says.

"If we come back," Screen Lock says.

"Guess there are worse things than being dirt-bound," Trip says. He turns to Lock. "But you... You giving up on your warplane empire so easily?"

"There are other types of empire to forge."

Trip arcs an eyebrow at Lock. "Now that the deck's clear, you're going to try and take over the world, aren't you?"

Lock smirks. "What, like that's not in your long range plan?"

CHAPTER TWENTY-TWO

"HONEY, I'M HOME!" Trip announces as he twitches the *Festering Wound* into park and kills the engine.

Rox, hands behind her, pressing on the small of her back, is waiting for Trip in front of Morty's three-story shack of a house as he gets out of the car.

"I take it you had something to do with that?" Rox asks, nodding up at the moon.

Trip looks up and smirks at the near-full orb, fresh letters carved into its face with satgun lasers.

KNOCK IT OFF ALREADY, BOZOS.
WE'RE WATCHING YOU.

"Maybe a little." Trip's smirk turns into a smile as he steps up to Rox, putting his hand behind her head and pulling her gently toward him for a long kiss. A minute later, they come up for air and he asks, "What's going on? The camps outside town were gone when we drove up."

Rox shrugs, shifting her weight from foot to foot. "War's over, the refugees are all returning home."

"More good news," Trip says. He puts a hand on Rox's belly, chuckles when he feels movement under the skin. "So why is everybody so dour? Come on, I saved the world, stopped the war, got the refugees to skedaddle. People should be throwing me a party."

"Nobody's in a party mood at the moment, Trip," Rox says, heading inside the house.

"Why? Somebody die?" Trip asks, following. "Was it me? Did I die?"

"Nobody died." Rox lowers herself into the first empty chair she comes across. "It's just—"

"War's over," Morty says. He's leaning back in a massive broken Laz-y-boy, his feet up on a metal folding chair, his bathrobe open, nothing on underneath. A giant mug of beer rests on his stomach. He sucks away at a hose of a straw.

"Yeah, know that," Trip says. "Hey, thought you'd gone sober?"

"War's over," Morty says, and the rest of the Sorta-council, scattered around the living room with their own beers and sour expressions, grunt in shared dismay.

"You say that like it explains something," Trip says.

"A couple hours after the war ended, the order cancelations started to come in," Rox says.

"War's over, and nobody wants our beer anymore," Morty mumbles at the ceiling. "Other priorities, they say. Rebuilding, they say. No time for beer."

Rox stands and walks over to her father, pulling his robe up to cover his crotch. "Don't get him wrong, he's thankful the war is over... we all are. But it's sort of crashing our economy."

"You did this!" Morty says, pointing a shaking finger at Trip.

"Ending the war, making me layoff all these fine people. And the grain, all that grain we imported... how are we going to pay for it now? It's gonna rot! Rot I say!"

"To be fair, it was mostly Lock and my granpap," Trip says. He grabs a milk jug off a table and fills Morty's mug. "Here, have another beer."

"Your granpap?" Rox asks. "You never told me you had a granpap."

Trip taps his temple. "Digital ghost inside my implant. Been hiding there all these years. Wonder if there's any way to get back rent from him? Anyway, you wanna blame somebody, blame the ghost and Lock. And you know something, I think she's going to try and take over the world. She might be *evil*."

Rox glares. "You're just now suspecting that?"

"So all of a sudden it's wrong to give someone the benefit of a doubt?" Trip asks. "But hey, now that the war's over and things are gonna settle down around here, if you wanted to go back to concentrating on just being Mother Superior, nobody would blame you. It's your true calling, and there are other people, some right in this room, that are more than capable — some would say overqualified, even — to take certain small responsibilities off your shoulders."

"Did you end the war just so you could be Minister of War again?"

"No. Not *just*. But let's not get lost searching for trees in a forest of ulterior motives. What's important is, I ended the war, and there's really no need for you to be Minister of War anymore, not when you have more important religious duties to attend to."

"It doesn't matter who ended the war," Hattie, the Minister of Sewage, croaks from the shadowy corner. "What matters is who's going to pay for the sewage improvements now?"

"Hey, silver lining, frog-man," Trip says. "Without the

refugees clogging up the pipes, is there really even a need for sewage improvements anymore?"

Hattie gets to his flippered feet, taking a second to steady himself, his beer sloshing out of its mug. "That's it! I've had just about enough of your stupid, stupid face!"

"You're seriously coming at me?" Trip's hand reflexively slips underneath his tux jacket to settle on the handle of his elephant pistol. "What are you going to do? Flipper me to death?"

Hattie growls out an "Arggh!" and rushes at Trip. Well, tries to rush. He's pretty fat, and wearing swim fins. And halfway there he hits a wet patch on the plywood floor. His flippered feet fly out from under him and he falls down, cracking the plywood with his ass.

Trip lets go of his pistol. "Can't even walk without falling down. What a joke."

"There's water on the floor, idiot," Hattie yells between painful groans, waving at the pool spreading out from Rox's feet.

"And you're wearing flippers. I'd think you'd be able to handle a little water..." Trip's voice trails off as he stares at the puddle. "Um, why is the floor wet?"

"That'd be me," Rox says, "I'm having a baby. Like, right now."

"Universe, I present to you Tripper Zaphod Alexander Shawn Burton diGriz the Fourth," a beaming Trip says, lifting the swaddled newborn up towards the ceiling of Rudy's shack.

Rudy stares at him from the Impala couch. "Dude, our last name isn't diGriz."

Trip lowers the newborn. "Shh, the universe doesn't need to know that."

"We are not naming him Tripper!" Rox yells through the Empire Strikes Back bedsheet curtain from the back room.

"Fine." Trip smiles at the little pink face in front of him, the blue eyes, the fine head of hair. He pokes his fingertip gently against the newborn's turned-up nose and swears he gets a smile back. "Caligula, then," Trip says proudly.

"Better!" Rox shouts back.

"I'll tell him," the long blonde Sister of No Mercy civil patroller called Dorris, stationed at the front door, says through a crack in the door at another patroller stationed on the outside. She closes the door and clears her throat. "Excuse me, Trip."

"That's Minister of War Trip to you, trooper."

"Well, Minister, there's a woman outside demanding to see you."

"How do you like that, bro?" Trip smirks at Rudy. "Word must already be out I'm back in charge, but gotta say, wasn't expecting the sycophants to be swarming me so quickly. Hope whoever she is she brought a lot of cash—there's a lot of lost bribe-time to make up for."

"She says she's your mom," Dorris says.

Trip's face goes grim. He holds his hand at chest height. "About this tall, red-haired, and well-armed?"

"Extremely well-armed," Dorris says.

"That's mom, all right." Trip tucks little Caligula under his arm and turns to Rudy. "We gotta go. This place got a back door?"

ABOUT THE AUTHOR

J.I. GRECO is an author, doodler, amateur curmudgeon, and disposable fountain pen owner.

Visit his official website at:
wholesaleatomics.com

FREE STUFF

Subscribe to J.I. Greco's newsletter for email notifications about new releases, and get the prequel to *Take the All-Mart!* for free as a thank you. To sign up, visit wholesaleatomics.com and click on the FREE STORY link at the top of the page.

Printed in Great Britain
by Amazon

64651382R00085